# Tell the Stars

# to Shine

### Austin and Amber
### Summer Lake Seasons Book Six

## By SJ McCoy

A Sweet n Steamy Romance

Published by Xenion, Inc

Published by Xenion, Inc.
First paperback edition 2020
www.sjmccoy.com

This book is a work of fiction. Names, characters, places, and events
are figments of the author's imagination, fictitious, or are used
fictitiously. Any resemblance to actual events, locales or persons
living or dead is coincidental.

Cover Design by Dana Lamothe of Designs by Dana
Editor: Mitzi Pummer Carroll
Proofreaders: Aileen Blomberg, Traci Atkinson, Becky Claxon.

ISBN: 978-1-946220-71-4

# Dedication

*For Sam. Like stars in a sunlit sky. Few.*

*xxx*

# Chapter One

When she came out of the bakery, Amber hesitated. She could turn right and head straight back to Grandma Lenny's with the pastries or, if she went left, she could take a little detour down along the beach.

It'd been a while since she'd seen the beach. She swung the bag as she walked. Lenny would love the cupcakes. Amber tried to make sure that she ate properly and stuck to a healthy diet since the heart attack. But a cupcake every now and then wouldn't do any harm.

She smiled when she turned the corner and saw the water. It sparkled in the evening sun. The beach looked to be empty—just the way she liked it. She stopped and turned when she heard a strange sound coming from the trees at the edge of the parking lot. It was like someone was whimpering over there. She approached cautiously, feeling a little apprehensive, and at the same time, a little foolish. She'd probably find a bird or something—she hoped.

The sound grew more urgent as she got nearer, as if whoever was making it could hear her coming and was trying to attract her attention. Her heart raced in her chest. What on earth was going on?

She could see a hole in the ground and had visions of a newsreader on TV talking about a shallow grave. She pulled herself together. Whoever or whatever was in that hole wasn't dead—they were making even more frantic noises now. She stopped a few feet away and peered over the edge and let out a laugh when she saw a big dog scrabbling at the dirt, trying desperately to get out.

"Hey, fella! It's okay. How did you get in there? And more importantly, how are we going to get you out?"

The dog stopped scrambling, as if the sound of her voice calmed him—at least, it looked like a him; she'd apologize later if it was a her. He cocked his head to one side and looked at her, and then let out a long, sad whine.

"Don't worry. We'll get you out of there." She set the bag with the cupcakes down and laid her purse beside it.

The hole was maybe three feet deep—why on earth was there a hole like that? She couldn't even imagine—kids maybe? It wasn't a pertinent question at the moment. More importantly, she needed to know if the dog was going to trust her if she tried to help him—or if he'd turn on her. She knelt down and held her hand out for him to sniff. He licked it and looked up at her. Okay, then. She was going to take that as a good sign.

She got down in the hole with him. It was deep enough that her boobs were at ground level. She knew she'd be able to get out again, but she'd have to pull herself up and swing her leg over the edge to do it. She looked at the dog. He wasn't small. She couldn't tell what breed he was—a mongrel by the look of him—and probably over a hundred pounds if she had to guess.

She stroked his head and he leaned against her leg, panting heavily. The poor thing was obviously stressed out by his ordeal.

"We're going to get you out of here."

He looked up at her with trusting eyes.

"We are," she reassured him. "Will you let me lift you?" She liked dogs, but she'd never had one. She didn't know them well enough to know if he'd let her lift him or if he'd be more likely to bite her for trying. There was only way to find out.

She patted the edge of the hole. "We're going to get you up here, okay?"

He tried to jump up, but his paws scrabbled against the dirt, and he slid back down. She cupped her hands behind his butt and tried to lift him. He wriggled away and sat down.

She blew out a sigh. "You're going to have to work with me here, doggy. I want to help you, but you have to help me, too."

She patted the edge again, and he stood up. This time when she cupped her hands behind his butt and heaved, he managed to get his front paws up on the ground. Amber heaved again, and he pulled himself the rest of the way.

She swung her leg up and pulled herself after him, grateful that there was no one around to see her undignified exit.

Once she was out of the hole, she got to her feet and brushed herself down. It didn't do any good; she was filthy. So was the poor dog. He sat there staring up at her, panting—as if waiting for her to tell him what would happen next.

She let out a laugh. "Don't look at me like that. I don't know. Where are you from? Where are your people?" He wasn't wearing a collar, so she had nothing to help her. "You'd probably better come with me. Lenny might know who you belong to. And if not, I guess we'll have to call the shelter."

She picked up her purse and the bag of cupcakes. "Are you coming?"

The dog got to its feet and followed her.

Austin looked around the office. Everything was shut down for the night. Time for him to get out of here.

He pulled his cell phone out of his pocket when it rang. "Hey, Colt."

"Hey, bud. Just checking that we're still on for tonight."

Austin laughed. "You mean checking that I haven't forgotten?"

"Yeah. That. I know you get busy, and you can't control when people call you up and want a last-minute showing."

"I do. But not tonight. I've been looking forward to dinner with you guys."

"We've been looking forward to it, too. Especially, Sophie. She's been bugging me ever since she got home from school, wanting to know what time you'll be here, and how much longer she has to wait."

Austin smiled to himself. Sophie was a little sweetheart. "Well, you can tell her that I'll be there within the hour. I was about to leave the office when you called. I'm going to stop by the house before I come. I want to check on Dallas."

Colt laughed. "You can bring him with you if you like."

"No. Thanks. I love my little brother, but I've had enough of his company the last few days. I'm looking forward to my evening with you guys and Sophie."

"Okay. I get that. Just wanted you to know that he's welcome."

"Thanks, bud. I'll see you in a little while, and I'll bring a bottle of that Grenache for Cassie."

"Thanks."

Austin laughed. "Don't worry. I'm bringing beer for you."

Colt laughed with him. "Now I can say thank you and mean it."

"What about Sophie? I thought it'd be nice to bring her something. You know ... Cassie gets wine, you get beer and she gets … what? I don't know what she likes. I don't know if Cassie minds her having soda or …?"

"Aww. That's why you're her favorite, you know. You think of little details like that to make her feel special."

"I try."

"If you really want to, you could bring her one of those little bottles of apple juice. She loves that stuff. And you're right; Cassie tries to keep her away from too much soda. Only if you have the time though; she won't notice if you don't bring anything. She's just excited to see you. She can't wait."

Austin chuckled. "At least there's one girl in town who likes me and can't wait to see me, then."

"Don't give me that shit. I'd swear that there's another girl who feels that way. But if you won't ask her out …"

Austin made a face. "Yeah. I keep thinking I'm going to."

Colt laughed. "You've been saying that for weeks."

"I know. Anyway. I'm going to hang up. There's no point talking on the phone when I'll be there soon anyway."

"And we can talk about it then."

He could hear the smile in Colt's voice.

"Whatever. See you in a bit." Austin hung up.

~ ~ ~

Amber looked down at the dog as he trotted along beside her. He looked back at her with big trusting eyes.

"Don't look at me like that. I can't keep you, no matter how much I like the idea. You must belong to someone, and I'm sure they're worried about you. Lenny will probably know who your people are—she knows everyone in this town."

Not surprisingly, the dog didn't say anything.

Amber looked down at herself when they reached the cut through that would take them out onto Main Street. That would be the quickest way back to Lenny's, but she wasn't sure that quickest would be best in these circumstances. For starters, she didn't know how the dog would behave around traffic—he'd followed her quite happily to this point, but they hadn't passed any cars or people yet. Another consideration was the state they were both in. She was covered in dirt, her hands were filthy, and the dog looked as though he'd taken a mud bath.

No. She made her decision and turned into the alleyway that ran along the back of the stores. It wouldn't be as quick as taking Main Street itself, but it ran parallel, and they should run into fewer possible problems back here.

The dog looked up at her and quickened his pace.

"Don't you run off on me now, will you?" She hurried to keep up with him, but his tail had started to wag, and he let out a sharp bark and took off.

"Ugh, great!" She watched him go with a sigh. What was she supposed to do now? He didn't go far. He ran past the next few yards and then stopped at a gate that led to the back of one of the stores. Amber couldn't work out which one it might be. They were out near the end of the downtown section of Main now. It could be one of the stores or perhaps one of the offices. She didn't know.

She got the feeling that she was about to find out as the dog nosed at the gate and then disappeared into the yard.

When she got there, she held the gate open with one hand but stayed out in the alleyway. She didn't like the idea of trespassing, even if was for a good cause.

"Come on, doggy. Let's go."

The dog turned and barked happily at her.

"No. I'm not coming in. You need to come out," she told him.

He wagged his tail and started nosing at a wooden box that stood near the back door.

Amber blew out a sigh when one side of the box opened inward, and the pesky dog went inside. She was going to have to rescue him again.

She looked around as she entered the yard, hoping that whoever it belonged to was an animal lover—and an understanding one at that.

She pushed open the side of the box and frowned when she found that the dog was nowhere to be seen. What the …?

She straightened up and had to step back quickly to get out of the way when the door flew open.

"Dallas! What the fuck are you playing at? You were supposed to keep him at … Oh!"

It took Amber a moment to catch her breath, though whether that was from the angry outburst or the guy who made it, she wasn't sure. Austin. Her heart hammered in her chest. Of all the yards the pesky dog had to go into, it had to be Austin's. Austin whom she'd had a crush on ever since she came to the lake. Austin who gave her butterflies. Austin who was now looking very confused … and who probably deserved an explanation.

"I … I'm so sorry."

He shook his head, looking even more confused. "I'm sorry. I didn't mean to yell at you. I thought …"

"It's okay. You have every right to yell at me. I'm out here lurking in your yard, but it's only because I was bringing the dog home with me to …" She glanced at the box—into which the dog had apparently disappeared. How was she going to explain that?

"You brought Roscoe home?" He frowned. "Are you with Dallas?"

It was Amber's turn to frown back at him. "Roscoe? You know him? And who's Dallas?"

They both turned at the sound of whining coming from the box. "You know you can't get back out this way buddy. You have to inside. Go inside, Roscoe."

Amber looked up at him. She couldn't help it. He was so handsome. He had kind eyes and a kind smile. He wasn't smiling at the moment, though.

"Dallas is—" Just as he started to speak, the back door flew open again. Austin wasn't as quick to get out of the way as she'd been and the force of the door hit him in the back, making him step forward and collide with her.

All the air rushed out of her lungs as she found herself trapped between Austin and the wall. She felt dazed. The way his body felt against hers left her light-headed.

He looked down into her eyes, and for one crazy moment, she'd swear that he felt it, too—that he wanted to close the short distance between their lips and kiss her.

"Dude! I am so sorry!"

Austin held her gaze a moment longer before he pushed himself away from her and turned toward the voice.

"Dallas! What the fuck is going on?"

Amber looked at the guy standing outside the back door. She'd heard mention that Austin had a younger brother before, and even if she hadn't known his name, it'd be easy to figure out who he was by looks alone.

He gave her a knowing smile. "I could ask you guys the same thing. I thought you'd be as worried as I've been about Roscoe. I didn't expect to find you making out in the back yard."

Amber felt her cheeks color. Was that what he thought was going on?

Austin glowered at him. "You've got a lot of explaining to do, D. You were supposed to be watching Roscoe at the house. Why did he show up here covered in dirt?"

Dallas shrugged and gave them an apologetic smile. "We came into town. I thought he'd like a bit of a walk, you know? But he took off, and I couldn't find him. I've been worried sick. I didn't want to come and tell you that I'd lost him. Did he just come back here by himself?"

Amber made a face at him. "No. He didn't. When I found him, he was stuck in a hole near the beach. The poor thing couldn't get out."

They both stared at her.

"Damn, I'm sorry." Dallas looked upset.

"Thank you," said Austin. "What do you mean, though, he was stuck in hole?"

She shrugged. "Exactly what I say. I don't know who'd been digging or why, but it was deep enough that he couldn't get out—and that I had trouble getting us both out once I got in there with him." She looked down at herself. "I don't usually go walking around town covered in mud."

Dallas gave her an odd look. "You're Amber, right?"

She nodded.

"Okay." He looked at Austin. "I'm going to take Roscoe home and give him a bath. I know you're out tonight. I'll take care of him."

Amber didn't understand the look the two brothers exchanged. Austin looked as though he was about to argue, but reluctantly changed his mind. "Okay. I'll see you back at the house. And you can pick me up a small bottle of apple juice on your way there."

"Just one?"

Austin nodded.

"It was nice to meet you, Amber." Dallas grinned at her, then disappeared back inside.

"You too," she spoke to the space he'd just vacated.

"I'm sorry about that," said Austin.

She could only hope that he was apologizing about Dallas or even Roscoe—and not about the way he'd unintentionally invaded her personal space before his brother appeared. There was no need for him to apologize for that—as far as she was concerned, he was welcome to do it again, anytime. In fact, starting right now would be nice. She had to pull herself together! He wasn't interested.

"That's okay. I'm just glad he's home now. He's a good dog. I'm glad I found him."

"Not as glad as I am." He ran a hand through his hair, and Amber's fingers twitched at her sides, wishing that she could do the same.

"Dallas means well, but he's not the most responsible guy." He was looking at her now, looking her up and down.

Her body responded to him and she bit down on her bottom lip wishing that he was looking at her the way she imagined he was. Then it dawned on her—she was covered in dirt! He was just noticing what a mess she was. Damn! She bent down and picked up the bag with the cupcakes from where she'd set it on the ground when she'd tried to figure out where the dog—Roscoe—had disappeared to.

She straightened up and smiled at him. "Well, excitement over, I guess. I wish I'd known he was your dog."

Austin shrugged. "I don't like to bring him around people too much. He's not always the friendliest. We do fine at home, but he's not big on strangers, and with my job, there's a lot of dealing with strangers."

She nodded. She knew he didn't consider her a stranger; they were part of the same group of friends, but they weren't exactly real friends either. "Well, he's okay. And that's all that matters in the end. I should get going."

She started toward the back gate, but he caught her arm. The feel of his hand on her made her breath catch in her chest.

Apart from that little close encounter up against the wall a few minutes ago, this might be the first time he'd touched her. It was only a hand on her arm, but her body reacted as if it were something much more intimate than that.

"Let me give you a ride home?" His hazel eyes seemed to sparkle gold and green as she looked into them. "It's the least I can do."

She held his gaze for a moment. She could think of a whole lot more that she'd like him to do, but that wasn't what he meant. She made herself relax and smile. "Thanks."

# Chapter Two

"So, err, how have you been?" Austin felt dumb as soon as the question was out. Surely, he could come up with something to talk about instead of just exchanging meaningless pleasantries.

She smiled and waited for him to unlock the door of his SUV. "Fine thanks. Lenny's doing much better. I'm spending more time in the post office than in the house these days. Oh, and I'm going to her place now; I'm having dinner with her."

Austin let her in and then hurried around to the driver's side to join her. He knew how well Lenny was doing—she was back to normal after her heart attack; at least, that was what she claimed. What he didn't know was what Amber and her sister, Jade's, plans were now. They'd come to Summer Lake to take care of their grandmother. But they'd seen her through the tough part, taking care of both her and the post office that she ran. He often wondered how long they planned to stay.

He glanced over at her, wondering whether he should ask. He remembered the first time he'd seen her—when she and Jade had come into his office looking to rent a place. He'd been bowled over by her. He shouldn't have been. He was still with Nadia at the time. But Amber had turned his head right around, and he hadn't been able to get right with himself since.

She gave him a puzzled smile. "What?"

Shit! He'd been staring at her. Thinking about the first time he'd seen her. And thinking about how beautiful she was. He smiled back. "Sorry. Nothing. I was just wondering …" Was he really going to ask her? Yeah. He'd never get a better opportunity. "I don't mean to be nosey or anything, but I was wondering how long you and Jade plan to stay."

He wished he hadn't asked when her smile faded.

"Sorry. It's none of my business."

"No! It's okay. It's not that I mind you asking; it's just that I don't know the answer. Lenny says she's fine to do for herself now—and she is, mostly. But I hate the thought of leaving and her being all alone." She frowned, and Austin guessed that there were other reasons she didn't want to leave, but he knew better than to think that he might be one of them.

"I guess all you can do is play it by ear."

She nodded. "I'm sorry. Am I being dumb, here? Are you trying to figure out how long we're going to want the apartment?"

"No!" He'd rented them the best apartment he had—the top floor of one of the buildings out on the airport road. He'd given it to them at a better price than he would anyone else, too. But if she—if they—wanted to stay there forever, he'd be more than happy. "No. I'm not worried about the apartment." He started up the engine, realizing that he probably shouldn't keep her here talking all night, no matter how much he might like to. "I was curious if you plan to stay."

She glanced over at him, but he kept his gaze fixed on the road as he pulled out. When she didn't say anything, he wished that he'd just come right out and asked the question rather than told her that he was wondering about it.

After a little while, she blew out a sigh. "To be honest, I don't know what I'm going to do. I should go home."

His heart was racing. He didn't want her to leave town. He wanted her to stay. He'd wanted to ask her out ever since he and Nadia broke up, but at first he'd felt like he should give it a decent amount of time, and then since that time had clearly passed, he'd kept chickening out. Maybe this was it? Maybe if he didn't ask her now, she'd leave, and he'd never get the chance again.

"Do you want to go home?"

She shook her head rapidly. "No! I'd love to stay here, but …" She shrugged. "My parents' business … I used to help with the books."

"Do they need you back?" He'd understand if her family needed her.

"No. The work isn't exactly rocket science. They could hire someone else to come in and do it, but he refuses to."

That was an odd way to say it. Perhaps her father wanted her to come home?

She smiled. "If it's up to me, I'll be here for a long while yet."

Austin chose to take that as confirmation that he should ask her out. If he didn't do it in the next couple minutes, they'd be at Lenny's, and it'd be too late again. "I'm glad to hear it."

She looked over at him.

"I'm glad to hear it because I've been wanting to ask—" His phone started to ring and cut him off mid-sentence. He just could not catch a break when it came to Amber.

She smiled. "Go ahead; take it. Don't mind me."

No way was he going to take the call. It could wait. The trouble was, it'd interrupted the moment. He turned onto Lenny's street.

Amber picked up her purse and the bag. "Thanks for the ride."

Damn! She was going to get out, and he wasn't going to get the chance to ask her. "Thank you for rescuing Roscoe."

"The pleasure was all mine. He's a good boy."

Austin nodded. "He is."

She reached for the door handle. It was now or never.

"I guess I'll see you around."

He nodded again. He'd failed again. "Are you coming out tomorrow night?" he asked as her feet hit the ground.

"I think so. I think we're meeting up with Ally. Angel said everyone's going. Will you be there?"

"Yeah."

"Okay. I guess I'll see you then, then."

"I guess so. Can I buy you a drink … as a thank you?"

She laughed. "There's no need. Like I said, I enjoyed meeting Roscoe."

"I'd like to." He held her gaze for a moment, hoping that she might understand that he wanted to do more than say thank you, even if he was screwing this up.

Her expression changed. He hoped that was a good sign, but he wasn't sure. "Okay, then, thanks."

He watched her walk up the path to Lenny's front door. Jeez. Logan would give him some grief if he'd witnessed that little exchange. How to mess up asking a girl out in three easy steps! His only consolation was that he'd bought himself the chance to try again tomorrow night.

He checked his watch and pulled away. He needed to get moving. He didn't want to be late to Colt and Cassie's.

Amber let herself into Lenny's and leaned back against the door. Phew! That was the first time she'd been alone with him. He always made her feel a little bit stupid, but jeez! She'd been tongue-tied the whole ride. Talk about awkward conversation! Still, he hadn't raced away as fast as he could, like she'd expected him to. No, he'd asked if she was going out tomorrow night—asked if he could buy her a drink. She pressed her lips together but couldn't hold the smile in. Did that mean …? It kind of felt like it did. The way he'd looked at her seemed as though he was saying that he wanted to buy her a drink, as in a kind of date type thing. She pushed away from the door. Or did it? Was she just getting carried away?

"Is that you, Amber?"

"Hey, Grandma. It is. Sorry it took me a while." She went into the kitchen and found Lenny slicing strawberries.

"No problem. There's no set time for anything in my house, you know that." Lenny's expression changed when she looked up. "Good Lord! What happened to you?"

It took Amber a moment to understand, then she looked down at herself and laughed. "Oh! Sorry. I forgot. I'm filthy. I should get washed up."

"What happened? Are you all right?"

"I'm fine. It was funny really. I found a dog in a hole."

Lenny raised an eyebrow.

"Someone dug a huge hole by the trees at the edge of the parking lot—you know, down by the beach? Well, I heard whimpering, and I had to see what was going on. I ended up getting down in there with him to get him out."

"And where's this dog now? Did he run off?"

Amber shook her head. "You won't believe this. I was bringing him back here with me, thinking you'd know who he belonged to, but he ran off. I followed him, and it turns out that he belongs to Austin. Apparently, his brother's in town and was supposed to be watching Roscoe for him."

Lenny chuckled. "That sounds about right. Austin's the responsible one, Dallas is ..." She shook her head with a smile that said while she might disapprove of Dallas, she had a soft spot for him. "Dallas is another story altogether." She met Amber's gaze. "Which one of them do you like better?"

Amber felt the heat in her cheeks. Jade and Lenny had teased her about her crush on Austin often enough. "Do you really need to ask?"

"I hoped not. I like Austin for you, but Dallas ... no. He's different. If anything, the difference between those boys is like the difference between you and Jade."

"I can see that. I only met Dallas for a few minutes, but ..." She rolled her eyes. There was no point trying to hide anything from Lenny, and she didn't even want to. It was nice to have someone to talk to about how she felt. "He's no Austin, is he?"

Lenny laughed. "He isn't. And now you know Roscoe, too. If I'd known you were planning to climb into a hole to rescue him, I would have been scared to death. That dog doesn't have the best reputation."

"Austin said he doesn't often like strangers."

"There's an understatement. I have to call Austin when we have a package for him that won't fit in the mailbox. None of my guys will deliver anything to the house because of Roscoe."

"Really? I was a bit concerned at first, but he was a sweetheart with me."

"Dogs know." Lenny smiled. "Anyway, you go and get cleaned up, and I'll finish fixing dinner."

"Thanks." Amber held up the bag. "I brought cupcakes, though I'm not sure what shape they'll be in."

"The shape won't affect the taste." Lenny took the bag. "Go on. Wash your hands at least. It's not often I see you with a hair out of place."

Amber smoothed her hair down, self-consciously.

"Leave it be. I'm not criticizing. I'm pleased if anything. It'll do you good to loosen up a bit—and if you're going to start getting dirty, I can't think of a better guy than Austin for you to do it with."

Amber had to laugh, even as she felt her cheeks flush again. "I wouldn't mind, but he's still not shown any interest."

Lenny's smile faded. "Really? Not even after you rescued Roscoe?"

Amber shrugged. "Well, he gave me a ride back here ... and he did ask if I'll be out tomorrow night ... Okay, will you tell me what you think this means?"

"What?"

"He asked if I'll be out tomorrow night, and when I said yes, he asked if he could buy me a drink. Does that mean ...?"

Lenny grinned. "I believe it does. I've told you all along. He's interested. It's written all over his face whenever I've seen the two of you around each other. But when you first arrived, he was still with that little bitch, Nadia."

"Yes, but he broke up with her a while ago ..."

"True, but would you have wanted him to dump her and come straight to you?"

Amber shook her head.

"That's right. He's a good boy." Lenny stopped herself and smiled. "You have to remember; I've known him since he was a baby. He's not a boy. He's a good man. You should be glad he's taken his time and put a respectable distance in between ending things with her and starting things with you."

"But he hasn't started anything with me."

Lenny chuckled. "We'll see if you can still tell me that on Saturday morning."

Amber smiled at herself in the mirror above the sink while she washed her hands. She'd love to think that tomorrow night might be the start of something between Austin and her. Her smile faded; her parents probably wouldn't love it, though.

Dallas came out onto the front porch to meet Austin when he got home. "I was going to apologize, but maybe you should be thanking me?"

"Don't push it, little brother, don't push it."

Dallas grinned. "Okay. I won't—for now. But, if you don't ask her out soon, then I will start pushing it. She's into you—it's obvious. Just get on with it."

"You think so?" He regretted the question as soon as it came out.

To his relief, Dallas nodded seriously. "I'd wondered if perhaps you were lusting after some chick who wasn't interested. But that's not the case. You say the word, and she'll—"

"Don't!" Austin didn't want to hear whatever Dallas might come up with—that wasn't to say he wouldn't wish that she'd do it, but he couldn't have his brother talking about her that way.

Dallas waggled his eyebrows. "I'll let you fill in the blanks for yourself, but since you asked, yes, I do think she's into you. In fact, I'd put money on it. So, would you stop being such a decent guy and get on with it? I'm telling you; she'd be happy to get indecent with you."

Austin pursed his lips.

"Go on, smile about it!" Dallas laughed. "Though if I were you, I wouldn't have come home alone."

Austin blew out a sigh. "The thought had crossed my mind. But it kind of goes with being a decent guy. I already made plans with Colt and Cassie tonight." He checked his watch.

"I'm pushing it now. Please tell me you didn't forget the apple juice."

"I didn't. It's in the fridge. What's the deal with that?"

"It's for Colt and Cassie's little girl—I'm taking beer for him, wine for her, I didn't want to leave Sophie out."

Dallas shook his head. "You're going to make someone a wonderful wife someday."

"Don't start. Not all girls are looking for a bad boy who'll treat 'em mean and keep 'em keen, like you."

"You're right. Can I do anything?"

"No. Thanks. Just stay home tonight—you and Roscoe?"

"Sure. We're planning on pizza and a movie."

"Just don't let him have too much pizza."

"Yes, Mom."

Roscoe came to greet them as they went inside. Austin scratched his ears. "I can't stick around tonight, bud. But don't go getting yourself into any more trouble, okay?"

Roscoe looked up and panted at him.

"Don't worry. We'll be good," said Dallas.

It was only a few minutes after seven when Austin pulled into Colt and Cassie's driveway. He loved that the two of them lived here now. It had been Cassie's childhood home when they were all in high school.

As soon as he cut the engine, Sophie came running down the front steps. "Uncle Austin, Uncle Austin. You're here! I thought you were never going to come."

She wrapped her arms around his waist as soon as he got out of the SUV. "Sorry I made you wait."

"And he's only a few minutes late." They both turned to see Colt smiling at them.

"I know," said Sophie. "But I haven't seen you for ages, and I want you to come down to the beach with me and help me find some more pink stones."

Colt winked at him over her head. "Maybe after dinner, but you know Cassie wants us to eat first. Why don't you go and wash your hands?"

Austin felt her little arms tighten around his waist. Then she looked up at him and made a face. "Promise? After dinner? He's just trying to get you out of it."

He had to laugh. "I promise."

She ran back inside the house, and Colt came to take the beer he got out of the back.

"They should still be cold."

"They are, and I have some anyway." Colt raised an eyebrow at him. "Are you okay?"

"Of course. Why?"

"I don't know. You seem ... ruffled?"

"No." He smiled. "Well, maybe a little."

"Why?"

He had to tell Colt. "Because a lot's happened since I talked to you earlier. And I kind of asked Amber—"

"You finally asked her out? Awesome!"

"Hmm. Kind of."

"What does that mean?"

"I asked her if she was going out tomorrow night. And she is. So, I asked her if I could buy her a drink ... does that count as asking her out?"

Colt chuckled. "I suppose it could—in your world at least. The important question is, did she understand what you meant?"

He shrugged.

Colt grasped his shoulder and steered him toward the house. "Then, if you ask me, tomorrow night, you're going to have to make what you meant very plain to her." He grinned. "Then again, I'm almost as bad as you are when it comes to women. Maybe we need to ask Cassie."

Austin laughed. "Probably. She'll set me straight."

# Chapter Three

Amber rubbed a towel through her hair as she came out of the bathroom and went to knock on Jade's bedroom door. "Are you up?"

"I'm thinking about it."

"Well, the bathroom's free."

"Thanks. Did you make coffee yet?"

Amber laughed. "What would you do if I said no?"

The bedroom door opened, and a bleary-eyed Jade groaned. "I might actually die."

"Then it's a good thing I did, isn't it? Come on, I'll fix you a cup."

"That's okay. I can do it."

"I'm going to make myself one. I may as well do yours, too."

"Thanks, sis." Jade padded after her into the kitchen. "You're too good to me."

"I know."

"I was thinking, do you want to take the day off? Lenny doesn't need both of us, and you haven't had a break in weeks."

Amber frowned. "Are you looking to butter me up so that I'll owe you one when you want to take off?"

Jade gave her a hurt look. "I want to be offended, but I don't suppose I can really. You know me too well. But, no, hard as it

24

might be to believe, I worry about you. You haven't had any fun since we've been here. I thought coming to the lake was going to be just what you needed. But nothing's changed; you're still so responsible and …" She shrugged. "I'm not criticizing. Don't think that. I just want to see you happy, and I thought coming here—and getting away from him—might make you happy."

"It has! I am! Honestly, Jade. I love it here. I'm happy." She poured two mugs of coffee and Jade sat down at the counter. "I know I'm not out having a wild time or anything, but I'm enjoying life here."

"I know you're enjoying taking care of Lenny—as much as she'll let you—but that's about all you've got going on."

"That's not true. I go out as much as you do."

"Yeah, but only because you go out when I do. You haven't made any friends … or met a guy."

Amber tried to hide her smile.

Jade laughed. "You get that look on your face every time you even think about him! But Austin doesn't count. Sure, you met him, but he's as bad as you are. Not a single date in … how many months have we been here?"

"Maybe that's about to change."

Jade blew out a sigh. "We've thought that since he broke up with what's-her-face but—"

"Hear me out, would you? I didn't get the chance to tell you last night, but I ran into him—"

Jade leaned forward eagerly. "And …?"

"And it's a long story—"

"But he asked you out?"

Amber bit her lip. "Kind of. I think."

"For crying out loud, Amber! He either did or he didn't. There is no kind of."

"You tell me which it is, then. I found his dog last night and ended up taking him back to Austin's office. He gave me a ride back to Lenny's afterward, and before he dropped me off, he asked if I'd be out tonight. When I said I would, he asked if he could buy me a drink." She stared at her sister and waited. Jade had much more experience with guys than she did. She'd know whether it counted as asking her out—as a date—or not.

Jade took a sip of her coffee. "What else did you guys talk about while he was driving you home?"

"Not much. It was kind of awkward, to be honest. He asked after Lenny, and how long we plan on staying here, and ... that's about it. Well, he said there was something he'd been wanting to ask me for a while, but then his phone rang and then we got to Lenny's and ..."

Jade smiled. "Going off that, I'd guess that the thing he's been wanting to ask you is if you'll go out with him."

Amber couldn't help bouncing up and down on her toes. "You think so?"

Jade laughed. "I do. I've always thought he liked you, but I couldn't figure him out. I think he's like you. He's more responsible and takes his time to do things right. But yeah. If you add it all up; he asked how long you're going to be here, said that there's something he's been wanting to ask you, and asked if you'll be out tonight and if he can buy you a drink ..." She nodded. "That sounds like a date to me."

Amber hugged her chest. She couldn't help it. "Then you have to help me figure out what to wear."

"No way." Jade shook her head resolutely. "He likes you—because you're you. I'll help you get ready. I'll do anything I can, anything to help you be more you. I like Austin. He's nothing like Milo. But if you're going to start going out with him, then we want to be sure that he's with you for who you are—not because I made you look like someone else, or because of what he thinks he can get out of it."

The happy excitement in Amber's chest fizzled out at the mention of his name. "Austin's not like that. He's nothing like him."

"I know. I'm sorry. That was probably overkill. It's just when you asked me to help you get ready, it took me back to when you two first got together. I still feel bad."

"It was hardly your fault."

"I still feel like it was. But let's drop it. We'll do your hair and your makeup your way tonight, and I refuse to lend you any of my clothes. Okay?"

Amber smiled. "Okay, deal. I'm beyond that anyway. I've learned a lot since then."

"Good. And I hope you told Austin that you plan to stay here—for good?"

"How could I? You know Mom and Dad want me to go back."

"They want you to be happy! Milo's the one who wants you to go home because he thinks he can get you back if you do. You make his life easier. When you're there you do more of the work than he does, and he takes all the credit and jokes about you being his little woman who does the books."

"I know. Can we forget about him?"

"We can. As soon as you tell the folks that you're not going home. That that lazy shit needs to hire someone to replace you. Once you do that, you can forget all about him and get on with living a happy little life here."

"I want to, I really do."

Jade blew out a sigh. "I need to get in the shower, or I'm going to make us late. Let's take it one step at a time, shall we? Today, we help Lenny. After work, we prepare you for your big date, and then tonight …" She waggled her eyebrows, "you could ask Austin to help you move on."

"I couldn't ask him that, it'd mean telling all about—"

Jade set her mug down on the counter and got to her feet. "I meant you could sleep with him!"

"Oh!" Amber felt dumb.

Jade wrapped her in a hug. "Sorry. I shouldn't tease you like that. I think you and Austin will have a good time together. And for what it's worth, I don't think he's the kind of guy who'd want you to go to bed with him on the first date."

"Neither do I."

Jade grinned at her. "And that's just one of the many reasons that you're so taken with him, right?"

She nodded happily.

~ ~ ~

Diego slapped Austin on the back as they came out of the title office. "Thanks for all your help."

"It's been my pleasure. I'm sorry it took longer than I first expected."

"That was hardly your fault." Diego smiled. "I believe everything works out as it should, in its own time."

Austin nodded. He had a sudden urge to ask the older man why he believed that. Diego had just closed on a house here. He had a new woman in his life, and it sounded as though the two of them were about to get serious. It was hardly his place to ask, though. Diego was his friend Zack's dad, but Austin didn't know him that well. Perhaps, if they could sit and chat for a while Diego might be able to give him some advice before his date with Amber tonight. He needed all the advice he could get. His track record with relationships was less than stellar—and he wasn't even sure that Amber understood that this was a date.

"I'd like to think that, too. What do you say, do you want to come over to the Boathouse for a drink to celebrate?"

"Thanks, but no. I want to get back over to the lodge at Four Mile and bring Izzy back to see the house."

"Oh. She's with you?"

Diego nodded.

"I'll let you get going then."

"Thanks. Will you be out tomorrow night? Zack said everyone's coming over here."

"I will. Though I'm not sure how long I'll stay." He couldn't even think about what he'd be doing tomorrow night until he saw how tonight went—best case he might be taking Amber out again; worst case, he might just have to come out to show his face and let everyone know he hadn't died of shame after somehow screwing things up.

Diego laughed. "When I was your age, I'd have shut the place down every weekend. You're young and single, why not make the most of it?"

Austin didn't know how to answer that.

"Ah. You don't wish to be single anymore? Who is she?"

Austin laughed. "What makes you think that?"

"I can tell. I've watched guys fall by the wayside over the years when they got hooked by a woman." He smiled. "Now, I've fallen, too. I can see it in your eyes. Do you want to tell me about it?"

Austin was tempted to take him up on the offer to talk about it. But he shook his head; he couldn't be that selfish. "No. You need to get back over to Four Mile, pick up your lady, and bring her back to see your new house. You've got a new life to get started on. You don't need to be hanging around here, listening to my woes. I appreciate the offer, though."

Diego grasped his shoulder. "Promise me that if you need someone to talk to … someone older." He smiled. "I can't claim wiser, or even more experienced …"

Austin raised an eyebrow at that. Everyone knew that Diego had a way with the ladies. Even the girls Austin's age went gaga over him.

Diego chuckled. "In matters of the heart. If you're looking for something less complicated, then I'm your expert."

Austin laughed. "Thanks. I might take you up on the offer someday soon." Diego had a point; he wasn't looking for advice about how to be successful with the ladies in general, only with one in particular—he was interested in something meaningful with Amber, not looking for tips on how to get her into bed.

"You have my number. You know where I live. I'll help you any way I can, any time."

"Thanks. But for now, you need to get going. I'll no doubt see you around over the weekend."

He smiled to himself as he watched Diego hurry back to his car. He wanted to know what it must feel like to be at the beginning of a new chapter in life—to have bought a house and be about to move into it with the new woman in your life.

He gave himself a mental shake. He hadn't even taken Amber out for the first time yet. He needed to focus on that first.

He looked at his watch. Diego's closing was the last appointment he'd had scheduled for the day. He had nothing but time on his hands until he came out tonight. He wished that he'd asked Amber if he could pick her up. But he hadn't. He knew he'd messed the whole thing up—he could have done so much better. But at least he'd left himself a thread to pull.

It was only three-thirty. He could go back to the office and catch up on some paperwork—there was always plenty of that to do. But no. It was Friday afternoon. He'd rather go home and take Roscoe out for a walk—and see what Dallas was up to.

~ ~ ~

"Will I do?" Amber turned to check out her back view in the mirror.

Jade laughed. "Yes, your ass looks great!"

"Well! Why shouldn't I want to look nice?"

"I'm not saying you shouldn't. I'm thrilled."

"I might not be as outgoing as you are, but I'm not some shy little virgin."

"Oh, I know."

"Good. I know you feel sorry for me because of the whole Milo thing. But, if you remember, before him, I used to know how to have a good time. I used to date."

"I don't feel sorry for you. I just feel protective of you. I don't think you're a victim or anything. You just got manipulated by an asshole. That's all—it happens."

Amber met her gaze. "Not to you. You'd never have allowed yourself to get stuck in that situation."

"No." Jade looked serious, but then she laughed. "Maybe that's because I am a manipulative asshole?"

"You are not. You're just strong-willed that's all."

"Yeah. But this isn't about me, it's about you. Are you happy with your outfit?"

Amber checked the mirror again and smiled. "I am." She was glad that summer had arrived. It stayed warm enough in the evenings that she could wear one of the strappy dresses she'd bought at Hayes. She wasn't skinny—not by any means—but she'd never wanted to be. And this dress reminded her why: it gave her an hour-glass figure. It showed off her ass—made it look great, just like Jade had said. And, in front, it did the same for her boobs—without showing too much or allowing them to bounce too freely.

Jade raised an eyebrow at her. "Penny for them?"

"They're not worth that much."

"Tell me anyway?"

"Honestly? I was thinking that I'm not that bad at all. In fact," she patted her hair and pouted, trying to make a joke out of it, "I'm quite attractive, if I do say so myself."

Jade wasn't fooled. "You're gorgeous! And you need to get rid of any lingering doubts or niggles that bastard left in your mind."

"I wasn't talking about him."

"I know. You were talking yourself back up after he tore you down."

"He never meant to. It's just the way he is. I truly don't believe he ever meant me any harm."

"You may be right. But I'm not interested in what he meant or how he is or in any kind of excuses. What matters to me is the effect he had on you. He stole your shine. And I hate him for that."

"Hate's a strong word."

"And I'm a strong woman."

Amber chuckled. "Believe me. I know. So does Milo. Thanks, Jade."

Jade shook her head. "There's nothing to thank me for. And can we forget about all that now? You're supposed to be getting excited about your big date."

Amber pursed her lips. "I am excited. But what if we're wrong? What if Austin only meant what he said—that he wants to buy me a drink to say thank you for rescuing Roscoe? What if …"

"Would you quit with the what ifs?" Jade began and then her expression softened. "Sorry. I don't believe that's the case— not for one minute. The guy lit up the moment he first laid eyes on you. But you're looking for reassurance, so I'll offer some. Worst case scenario is that he only wants to buy you a drink to say thank you. But when he sees you looking like that, he's not going to be able to resist. And if he's as slow off the mark as he has been up to now, then other guys are going to beat him to it. If he doesn't make it obvious that you're with him, other guys are going to make a move on you—don't look at me like that, I guarantee it. Then you'll both have a choice to make. Will he be prepared to fight for your attention—and will he still be the one you're interested in."

"He's the only one I'm interested in." She wasn't dumb; she knew there were other guys who'd ask her out if she gave them the chance—and some who wouldn't want to take her out but wouldn't mind taking her home. But she wasn't interested in guys. She'd been determined when she came here that she needed to be alone for a good while after everything that had happened with Milo. Austin was worth making an exception for—but he was the only one.

# Chapter Four

Austin made sure he got to the Boathouse early. He didn't want Amber to show up and wonder where he was.

"Hey, Austin. How's it going?" Kenzie, the bartender greeted him with a smile. "You're eager tonight, you're the first one of the gang here."

He smiled back at her. "I'm good, thanks. How about you? How are you and Chase doing?"

"We're great. I'm glad you're here, what can I get you? It's on me. If you don't mind me picking your brain for a few minutes while we're quiet." She laughed. "That sounded wrong. I'll still get you a drink even if you don't want me picking your brain."

"I'm fine with it, and I can get my own anyway. Your tab must be huge. You're always buying people drinks."

Kenzie shrugged. "It's the one thing I know that I can do for people."

Austin smiled. "They don't come to you for the drinks. They come for your wisdom."

She laughed out loud at that. "I am many things, bud, but wise isn't one of them. You want a glass of that Cab Franc you like?"

He nodded. "Thanks." Kenzie had had quite a troubled past from what he understood, but she'd been here in Summer Lake for a few years now, and in that time, she'd become a respected member of the community—someone who people sought out for advice. She wasn't one to sugarcoat anything. She told it like it was, and she'd helped a few of his friends figure their lives out when they'd needed it.

"I'm not going to argue with you—but only because I know I couldn't win. But if you still can't see yourself the way the rest of us see you …"

As she set his drink down, her smile told him that she knew what he meant, even if she didn't want to admit it. "Whatever. This is about me asking you for advice."

"Go ahead."

"It's about the house."

Austin had half expected it might be. She and her husband, Chase, had rented one of his properties for the last few years. "What about it?"

"Do you think they'd be interested in selling?"

Now, that, he hadn't expected.

"Aww. Don't look like that. Is that a no? We've been saving so hard and we have enough for a decent down payment now. We could look for somewhere else, but we both love that house." She smiled. "It's the first place that's ever felt like a home to me."

He held his hand up. "The look on my face wasn't a no."

"It wasn't? You think they might sell then?"

"They already did. I never even thought to mention it to you. It was a couple years ago. I knew you guys weren't in a position to buy it back then. I bought it myself."

Her eyes widened. "You're our landlord? As in, the owner, not just the manager?"

"Yep. I don't like to shout about it, but I buy quite a few of the properties I manage."

She gave him a shrewd look. "And do you ever sell any of them again?"

"Not usually."

She nodded sadly. "Okay. I get it. I had to ask. And I don't blame you. I bet you always won at Monopoly as a kid, didn't you?" She forced a smile. "I bet you bought up all the properties and stacked up a pile of cash."

He had to laugh. "You're only half right. I did buy all the property, and make bank, but I always used to feel bad for Dallas, and I'd lend him money and help him buy his own properties."

Kenzie laughed with him. "I should have known. You're too soft. And having met Dallas, I get it. He's a charmer, isn't he?"

"Something like that. But listen, Kenz. I'm not saying no about you guys buying the house. Let me think about it, okay? I'll put something together and give you a call. Maybe you and Chase can come in and see me toward the end of the week."

She frowned. "No. It's an investment to you. You wouldn't have bought it if it wasn't a good one."

"Exactly. To me, it's just an investment—and it's one of many. To you guys, it's home—and that is worth so much more than any amount of money." He felt bad when her eyes started to shine.

"Damn, Austin!" She sniffed loudly. "I always knew you were a good guy. But if you can make me fill up, you're something special." She pursed her lips, and he could see her chin tremble. "I need to go serve those guys who just came in. Don't go anywhere. I'll be right back."

He watched her dab at her eyes as she walked away. He knew it'd be a big deal to her and Chase, but he didn't know how to explain—without it coming off wrong—that it really wasn't a big deal for him. Sure, he'd done well for himself. Real estate was good business and had been getting better and better the last few years. He wouldn't deny that he enjoyed the financial success, but it wasn't what motivated him. What he loved about his job was exactly what Kenzie had just described— helping people find the place they would call home.

She surprised him when she came back—on his side of bar this time. She surprised him even more when she wrapped her arms around his shoulders and planted a kiss on his cheek. He looked up at her in surprise.

She gave him a bright smile. "I can't say anything because I'll get all emotional. But this ..." She pecked his cheek again. "Is my version of thank you."

"What's going on here, lover?"

They both turned to see Chase standing behind her with a puzzled look on his face.

Austin gave him an apologetic smile, but Kenzie just laughed. "Don't look like that." She wrapped her arms around him and gave him a kiss that made Austin feel like he should look away.

When they came up for air. Chase smiled at her. "Want to explain?"

She nodded at Austin. "I'll let him. I'll only cry if I try." She walked away to let herself back behind the bar.

Chase sat down beside Austin with a grin. "I'm guessing that if she's thanking you and kissing on you, you gave her some good news about the owners wanting to sell the house?"

He nodded. "Yeah. The owner, at any rate."

Kenzie set a beer down on the bar for Chase. "And Austin's the current owner!"

Chase grinned at him. "Awesome!"

Austin held up his glass, and Chase clinked his bottle against it. "We'll work something out." His smile faded and his heart started to race when he saw some of his friends coming in. Angel and Luke were with Roxy and Logan. He craned his neck to see if anyone else—anyone like Amber—was with them.

She wasn't.

Chase raised an eyebrow at him. "Are you waiting for someone?"

He smiled. "I hope so."

Kenzie rested her elbows on the bar and leaned forward. "Please tell me that you and Amber are finally going to get it on?"

He had to laugh at the way she put it. "I don't know about that, but I asked if I could buy her a drink tonight and …"

Kenzie's laugh made him feel kind of naïve. "Just get over yourself, would you? Buy her a few—and then take her home."

Chase chuckled and grasped Austin's shoulder. "That's not his style, Kenz. And it wouldn't be Amber's either. Do me a favor, lover, and don't do any of your usual style encouraging with these two?"

She gave him a sour look, but Austin gave him a grateful smile.

"Okay. I'll behave myself—if I must. But you'd better play a whole bunch of slow ones at the end of the night."

Chase smiled. "That I can do. And speaking of which, I'd better start getting set up. Eddie said he might be a bit late tonight."

~ ~ ~

Amber hesitated outside the door to the Boathouse before she pushed it open.

Jade stopped beside her and gave her an encouraging smile. "It's going to be a great night. Okay?"

She sucked in a deep breath and nodded. "Yeah. It is."

Ally leaned in next to Jade. "It is, Amber. Honestly. You look amazing. And I've told you before, Austin always looks at you as if he wants to eat you up."

She laughed. It was true; she said that all the time. Ally had only moved up here a little while ago, but she'd become a good friend very quickly. She was probably closer to Jade, but she'd insisted from the first time she'd met him that Austin had a thing for Amber.

At this point, all she could do was steel her nerves and go in there and find out.

Jade grinned at her. "And like I already told you, if he doesn't get his act together fast enough, some other lucky guy will." With that she pushed the door open and gave Amber a little shove.

As she walked inside, she set her shoulders back and held her head a little higher. Jade had been right earlier—Milo had left some lingering doubts in her mind, doubts about her own worth. And she knew she needed to move past them. If she didn't see herself as a catch, why should Austin?

She spotted him immediately. He was sitting at the bar with Ivan and Abbie—she liked them. She was glad he wasn't at the big table where most of the gang were already sitting. This was probably going to be awkward, at least, at first, and she was glad that whatever happened, it wouldn't happen in front of everyone.

"We're getting a drink first," said Jade and strode purposefully toward the bar.

Ally smiled at her. "Come on."

Austin looked up and caught her gaze. The way he smiled was enough to set her heart racing. He was such a good-looking guy. He was tall, maybe six feet, he wasn't all muscle-bound like some of their friends, but he had broad shoulders and big strong arms. She sucked in a shaky breath as she wondered how it would feel to have him close those arms around her.

To her surprise, he slid down from his stool and came toward her. His eyes never left hers.

Ally nudged her with her elbow. "I'm guessing that he's getting your drink."

Amber nodded. She tried to speak, but her throat was dry. Her heart beat louder in her ears with every step closer he came.

He stopped in front of her and looked down into her eyes. "Hi."

She had to swallow before she could reply. "Hi." She just kept looking into his eyes. They were doing that gold and green shimmery thing and it had her mesmerized.

The way he was looking back at her made it feel as though he was as dumbstruck as she felt. He smiled and let out a little laugh. "I wasn't sure if you understood what I meant last night—when I asked if I could buy you a drink."

She swallowed again and ran her tongue over her lips in an attempt to make her voice work. It didn't at first, so she nodded instead. "I wasn't sure if I did either." Her heart was hammering in her chest. Her palms were hot and sweaty, but instead of feeling nervous about him, she felt nervous with him. She'd expected to spend a while guessing whether she even had it right about this being a date. She hadn't thought that he'd be so open with her. She liked it. It made her feel close to him—like they were in this together, even if they were about to mess it up.

She smiled. "I hoped, but I didn't know."

His face relaxed. "You hoped?"

She nodded. He was putting himself out there, it was only fair that she should join him. "Come on, Austin. Surely, you've known for a while that I've been hoping."

She was thrilled to see a hint of pink touch his cheeks and his neck.

"I think I have to borrow your answer. I hoped, but I didn't know."

She smiled. "Well, now you know."

He put his hand on her shoulder, causing her to gulp for air as hot shivers raced through her. "Thanks, Amber. Now you know, too."

She nodded. She knew that she wanted to feel his hand on more than her shoulder!

"Can I get you that drink?"

She nodded again. "Yes, please."

He looked around. "Where did Jade go?"

She chuckled. "She and Ally probably skedaddled as fast as they could. You're stuck with just me."

He looked down into her eyes, and she felt the excitement bubble up in her chest again. "That's great."

When they reached the bar, Kenzie was waiting for them with a grin. Amber braced herself, expecting her to say something about them being there together, but she gave them a warm smile. "What can I get you, kiddies?"

Austin looked at Amber. "I'd like a glass of that Cab Franc, please."

Austin smiled. "Make that two."

She looked up at him; she'd forgotten that he was a wine guy. Most of the guys stuck with beer.

He smiled back at her. "Roscoe asked me to say hi."

She laughed. "He did? How's he doing after his little ordeal yesterday?"

"He's none the worse for it. And thank you again. I took a drive by the beach this morning and I saw the hole you were talking about. Thank God you found him." He shuddered. "He could have been stuck in there all night if you hadn't."

"Ugh. I didn't even think about that. I'm glad I found him, too."

Kenzie set their drinks on the bar and moved away again without a word.

Austin lifted his glass and held it out to her. She chinked hers against it. "What are we drinking to?"

He smiled. "To Roscoe. He finally made me do what I've wanted to do since the day we first met."

She smiled and bit down on her lip. She really hadn't expected him to be this open, but she liked it.

His smile faded. "Is it okay that I said that?"

"It is! I'm glad you said it, because it makes it easier for me to say that I've been hoping you would since the day we met."

The way he smiled at her made her insides turn to mush.

He rested his forearm on the bar, and she had to revise her opinion that he wasn't all muscly. She dragged her eyes away from it and looked up at him.

"Do you want to stay here at the bar, or would you rather find a table—or go join the others?"

She looked around. The others were all sitting at a couple of the big picnic tables—and half of them didn't manage to look away in time. She laughed. "It looks like we're the object of much curiosity over there—I'm not sure I want to brave it, but I will if you do."

He shook his head adamantly. "I'd rather find a table and have you all to myself; I just didn't want to assume."

She followed him over to one of the booths in the back.

"Is this okay?"

"It's great." She slid in and he sat opposite her.

He twirled his glass and then looked up at her. "I've waited all this time to ask you out, and now we're here I don't even know what to say."

She smiled. "If it's any consolation. I'm the same." She rested her hands on the table, suddenly afraid that this whole thing had just been a fantasy and that there would be no reality to back it up.

He soon changed her mind about that when he reached across the table and took hold of her hand. "I'm glad we're here, though."

Her heart started to race again. So was she.

# Chapter Five

Austin was feeling more relaxed as he led her out onto the dance floor. They'd gotten off to an awkward start, but soon they'd been laughing and telling each other stories about their lives—and their siblings.

A few of their friends had walked by their table during the course of the evening, but mostly they'd left them in peace. Though he'd felt several pairs of eyes on them. He knew there would be several more now that they were up to dance. It didn't matter.

What mattered was that Chase had caught him the last time he'd gone to the bar and told him that he planned to play a long section of slow songs at the end of the night—if he wanted to make the most of it.

He wanted to kiss her, but he wasn't sure that he wanted to do it here. He wasn't worried about who saw them, more about how she would feel about it. It was kind of a given around here—everyone knew that the couples out kissing on the dance floor at the end of the night were simply engaging in foreplay. That wasn't his plan. He just wanted to dance with her—get the chance to hold her.

He stopped and held his hands out to her. He had to close his eyes when she looped one arm up around his neck and rested her other hand on his chest.

He slid his arms around her waist, not daring to pull her too close against him.

When she looked up at him, her cheeks were flushed, and her eyes were bright. "Do you like to dance, or are just doing this for me?"

"I love to dance. I just don't often get the chance."

She frowned.

"What? What's the matter?"

"I probably shouldn't bring this up. But you never used to get up and dance when you were with … before."

He pursed his lips. He didn't like to remember the years that he'd spent with Nadia. "No. She didn't like to." He almost said that she didn't like to do anything that he enjoyed, but he thought better of it. He wanted to focus on Amber—and the future, not on Nadia and the past.

He held her a little closer, and she looked up into his eyes. "Were you miserable with her?"

Was it bad to admit it? It was better than lying, he knew that much. He nodded slowly. "I'm not blaming her. We hadn't made each other happy in a long time. I should have ended it sooner."

"I'm sorry. I know I shouldn't even be asking, but it feels like that's something we have in common."

He raised an eyebrow. "You stayed in a bad relationship too long, too?"

She blew out a sigh. "Far too long. I should never have gotten into it."

His arms tightened around her involuntarily at the thought of her with someone else. A thought struck him as he remembered their conversation from last night. "Did you work with him?"

She sighed. "Yeah. He works as the general manager for my parents."

"They have fast food franchises, right?"

"Yeah. A whole string of them. I used to do the books."

Austin's heart hammered in his chest. "Is he waiting for you to go home?"

"He is."

A wave of disappointment swept over him. He shouldn't even be dancing with her, let alone wondering about seeing her again.

She reached up and touched his cheek. "It's not like that. He wants me back. I don't want him back. I'm tired of being used."

He frowned. He wanted to ask what she meant but didn't feel like he had the right. Instead, he held her closer to his chest, loving the feel of her soft body pressed against him.

When she looped both arms around his neck and looked up at him, he couldn't help it. He lowered his mouth closer to hers and breathed, "You don't deserve to be used, Amber, not by anyone."

Her eyes locked with his, and she shook her head. "I won't be anymore, will I?"

"No." He brushed his lips over hers. "Not if I have anything to do with it."

She surprised him when she nipped his bottom lip. He'd been hesitant to kiss her, but she was eager. She cupped his cheek in her hand and kissed him hungrily. He'd been a gentleman, he was a gentleman, but there was no way he'd hold back from that. He ran his hand up her back and tangled his fingers in her hair as he kissed her.

When they finally broke away, he was finding it difficult not to let her feel the effect she was having on him. She bit down on her bottom lip but couldn't hide her smile. "I feel like I should say I'm sorry. I've never been this ... forward."

He chuckled and planted a peck on her lips. "Please don't say you're sorry. I'm loving it. And just to be clear, you can be as forward as you like with me."

To his surprise, she slipped her arms around his waist and then slid her hands down to cup his ass. "I can?"

He nodded eagerly. "Yep! Most definitely."

She raised an eyebrow. "Just so you know, I won't mind if you want to be forward with me, either."

Wow! His heart raced. If she was saying what he thought she was ... he couldn't do it. He rested his hands on her hips and pulled her against him, so that she could have no doubt about his attraction to her. "I'd love to," he said as her eyes widened, and her cheeks flushed. "But that's not who I am, and I don't think it's who you are, either?"

She gave him a grateful smile. "You really are a gentleman, aren't you?"

He chuckled. "I am. Right now, I want to say unfortunately, but I am. And if we're going to start seeing each other ..." He raised an eyebrow at her.

She smiled happily. "If that's you asking, then yes, I hope we are."

"Then I think it's best if we do it right. Take our time and be ourselves."

She stood up on her tiptoes and planted a kiss on his lips. "You're awesome."

He threw his head back and laughed. "And you are adorable."

Amber wasn't surprised to find her sister standing by the sinks when she came out of the bathroom stall.

"Well?" Jade asked eagerly. "It looks like it's going amazingly! I thought maybe he'd walk you home and kiss you goodnight—I thought that'd be a good result. I did not expect to see the two of you out there smooching your way through the erection section!"

Amber had to laugh. "The what?"

"Oh, my God! Don't tell me you've never heard the guys call it that?"

"The erection section? I haven't. What …?"

Jade groaned. "The slow songs, at the end of the night. When the couples get up and dance. When he gets to hold you against his boner for a while and let you know what he wants to do later."

"Oh, my God! I had no idea!"

"But … he did, right?"

"Partially."

Jade looked horrified. "He was only partially?"

Amber laughed out loud. "No! I mean yes, I felt it, but no he wasn't letting me know what he wants to do later. Well, he'd like to, but he's not in a hurry and neither am I."

"Aww. And he already said so?"

"Not in so many words, but yeah."

"So, will it be the walk you home and kiss on the doorstep? I can stay at Ally's."

"You don't need to do that."

"I don't mind."

"I'd rather you didn't. I'm not going to ask him in, and I don't think he'd come if I did. So, I'd rather you came home so we can talk afterward."

Jade grinned. "Okay. I can hang out here. Text when you're home and he's gone. Or if you change your mind let me know that he's not gone, so I don't walk in on you."

"That's not going to happen."

"Okay. You'd better get back out there. He'll be wondering what happened to you."

"Okay. I'll see you later."

"Have fun."

Amber made her way back out through the bar. She stopped when she saw a woman with dark hair standing beside the booth talking to Austin. Crap! It was Nadia.

She didn't know what to do. She should go and sit back down and see her off. But she didn't want to cause a problem—or a scene. It looked like Nadia had a lot to say for herself.

Amber jumped when someone slipped her arm through hers. It was Kenzie. "Come on, sugar. No way am I going to let her spoil your night." She strode toward the booth and towed Amber with her—whether she was ready to go or not.

Austin shot Amber an apologetic look, and Nadia turned to follow his gaze. Her eyes narrowed when she saw Amber.

"Hey, Nadia!" Kenzie let go of Amber. "I haven't seen you in here in ages. How've you been?"

Nadia looked taken aback but apparently, wasn't so hell-bent on making trouble that she didn't reply. "Fine, thank you."

"That's good to hear. You should come sit at the bar with me and have a drink. I was just coming to tell Austin that their cab's here."

Austin didn't miss a beat. He smiled gratefully at Kenzie and got to his feet. "Thanks, Kenz." He edged past Nadia and came to take Amber's hand. "Are you ready?"

She nodded.

Nadia shot Amber a venomous look, but Kenzie took her arm and started leading her toward the bar.

Austin gave Amber another apologetic smile. "I'm sorry about that. It seems she was pissed to see me out with you, though it's none of her business anymore."

She squeezed his hand. "It's all right. I understand. I've been there myself, but I didn't have a Kenzie to ride to the rescue. I didn't know she and Nadia were friendly."

He laughed. "They're not. Kenzie can't stand the sight of her. That was just for our benefit."

"Aww. She makes out she's a tough nut, but she's a sweetheart, isn't she?"

"She is." He gripped her hand a little tighter as they got closer to where the gang was sitting. "Do you want to stop and …?"

"No." She squeezed his hand right back. "Let's just go."

When they reached the door, he held it open for her and a rush of warm night air swept over her. It felt good.

"I'm sorry about Nadia."

"There's no need. Really. I understand."

"Thanks." He wrapped his arm around her shoulders and dropped a kiss on her lips. It was no big deal, just a casual gesture, but it felt special. It reinforced the feeling she'd had earlier that they were in this together. That was new to Amber. She'd only dated a few guys before Milo, but whenever she had, and especially with him, it'd felt like a minefield. As though a relationship was somehow adversarial. With Milo especially, she'd felt as though she was pitted against him with him looking to come out victorious and her just hoping to survive with her sense of self intact. With Austin it felt as though they were going in together and were helping each other figure out how it was supposed to work.

"I guess it was almost time to call it a night, but I wish she hadn't cut it short."

Amber nodded. She did, too. She didn't want this night to be over.

He hugged her closer into his side. "Do you want to take a cab, or should we walk?"

"I'd rather walk." At least, that way she'd get to enjoy his company for a little while longer. The apartment wasn't too far out of town. She frowned when she thought about it, though. "But then you'll have to walk back here again for a cab."

"It's okay. I'll call one when we get to your place."

"Oh. Of course."

They walked across the square, and she was surprised when he guided her toward the path that led down by the river.

He chuckled when he saw her face. "Don't worry. I'm not taking you down a dark lane—well, I am, but only because it's the prettiest way to get to your place."

"Aww. I wouldn't have thought to come this way."

"Good. I wouldn't want you to walk down here by yourself after dark."

Hearing him say that gave her the warm and fuzzies. But then she couldn't help comparing him to Milo again.

He gave her a puzzled look. "Was I wrong to say that? I know you're independent; you can do your own thing. I didn't mean to—"

"No!" She shook her head rapidly. "I don't mind. I like that you care."

"You looked as though you were mad at me."

"Not mad at you." She pursed her lips. They'd had the end of their evening cut short because of his ex, did she really want to spoil their walk home by talking about hers? She looked up at him, and the expression on his face told her that she probably should. She needed him to know.

"If I got a funny look on my face it was because I couldn't help comparing you to ..." She hesitated.

"Your ex?"

"Yeah. Except I don't like to call him that. He's not my anything. He's just the guy I used to be with."

He gave her a half smile.

"His name's Milo. And far from being mad at you for not wanting me to walk alone at night, I kind of liked it—a lot. And I couldn't help comparing you to him. Don't worry—you win hands down. There were a couple of nights when he sent me back for the cash box by myself."

Austin frowned.

"Yeah. You wouldn't want me walking around little old Summer Lake by myself. He sent me out at midnight to pick up the cash box that he'd forgotten—from the store in the worst part of Bakersfield ..."

Austin shook his head and his arm tightened around her shoulders. "I'm not going to say anything, but there's a lot I'd like to say."

She looked up at him. His jaw was clenched. "Say it if you like. I've heard worse from Jade."

"No. I will ask you something, though, if you don't mind."

"What?"

"You said he wants you back?"

She nodded, wondering what was coming.

He stopped walking and slid his arms around her waist as he looked down into her eyes. "I don't know what's going to happen between you and me—I don't want to say too much about that, it's too soon—but even if it's nothing. Even if you don't want to see me again, please promise me you won't go back to him, Amber? You deserve so much better than that."

Her heart felt as though it was melting in her chest as she looked back into his eyes. She put her hands on his shoulders.

"I promise you. I won't. I know better now." She smiled. "And besides, I do want to see you again."

He smiled back at her. "You do?"

"If you do?"

He nodded happily. "I do. Very much." He lowered his head and she lifted her lips to meet his. The way he kissed her left her sagging against him. When he'd kissed her earlier, out on the dance floor, it had been good, but she'd been aware of where they were and of the fact that people were watching. This was different. She stood in the warm circle of his arms, his soft lips brushed over hers, parting them, and then his tongue slid inside her mouth and started to explore. She clung to him and kissed him back hungrily. Her body heated up with desire, and she pressed herself against him, her hands roving over his back and shoulders. He made her want to take him home and not let him leave till morning!

When he finally lifted his head, he looked as dazed as she felt.

"Are you sure you're such a gentleman?" she asked with a half laugh.

The heat in the look he gave her sent arrows of excitement shooting through her veins. "Don't tempt me."

She wanted to.

He dropped a peck on her lips. "Please?"

She sighed. "Okay."

He took her hand, and they continued their walk back to her place.

~ ~ ~

As soon as they reached her building, Austin pulled his phone out of his back pocket. She gave him a puzzled look. He chuckled and dialed the cab company. He had to do it straightaway. He couldn't risk what would otherwise become inevitable when he kissed her again.

"Summer Lake Cabs."

"Hi, Bev. It's Austin. Can you send someone to pick me up out at 511 Hangar Lane?"

"Sure. Straight away?"

He glanced at Amber and nodded sadly. "Yeah."

"Okay, it'll be about ten minutes. Are you going home?"

"I am."

"Okay. It'll probably be Keith."

"Thanks."

He hung up and gave Amber a rueful smile.

"How long will they be?"

"She said about ten minutes."

Amber chuckled. "You think I'm a wicked woman who's going to try to seduce you, so you have to plan your escape?"

He slid his arms around her and looked down into her eyes. Hers widened when he held her closer. "No, I know I'm a wicked man who wants to seduce you. I'm planning my exit because I don't want to rush things between us."

"Would you think less of me if I said I wouldn't mind rushing?"

He chuckled. "Please don't tempt me."

"I had to try."

"I can't promise I'll have this much willpower tomorrow night."

"Tomorrow?" Her eyes widened, and she pressed against him eagerly, making him close his eyes and want to call Bev back to cancel the cab.

He opened his eyes and nodded. "If you want to see me again that soon?"

"I'd love to."

"Good. I'll come and pick you up this time. Now that I've got my act together."

She smiled. "I'd like that. What time?"

"Seven?"

She nodded happily. "Where do you want to go?"

He couldn't resist holding her a little closer still. But he did manage to stop himself from saying, to bed. "There aren't too many options around here. We could go for dinner at Giuseppe's. We could go back to the Boathouse." He wanted to add the option of her coming over to his place, but that probably wasn't a good idea, not if the last of his willpower was to stand any chance at all.

"Maybe Giuseppe's?"

"Okay. It's a date."

She laughed. "And this time I know it for certain."

He smiled. "And just so you don't have any remaining doubts that tonight was a date, we should probably end it with a kiss on your doorstep."

Her full soft breasts pressed against his chest as she lifted her lips to him. She kissed him back hungrily. He couldn't help filling his hands with her rounded ass—and as he did, he couldn't help wishing he were less of a gentleman.

# Chapter Six

Amber felt as though she floated through Saturday morning. She couldn't remember feeling this happy after a first date. In fact, she couldn't remember feeling this happy ever.

She was supposed to have had the morning off, but she'd woken up early and full of energy. She'd told Jade to sleep in while she went to help Lenny at the post office. It was only a half day on a Saturday anyway.

Once Amber had locked the front door after the last customer left, Lenny put her hands on her hips. "Don't think I'm going to let you leave here before you tell me all about it, young lady. I've been expecting you to bubble over with it all morning. You've held out on me so far, but I'm not letting you go until you tell me."

Amber laughed. "Is it that obvious?"

"To anyone with eyes in their head! You're all smiley and walking on air. I take it that it was a date?"

Amber nodded happily. "The best date I've been on in … well, maybe ever."

Lenny smirked. "And I know you won't want to admit this to your grandmother, but is the silly grin due to the fact that it wasn't just a date?"

Amber raised an eyebrow.

"Don't make me spell it out. Did the date not end when he took you home?"

"Oh!" She felt the heat in her cheeks. "No! I mean, yes! It did end. He didn't … we didn't …"

Lenny held her hand up. "Okay. You've answered. There's no need to say the words. And I'm sorry; I shouldn't have asked. But I thought that must be the only explanation. So, I had to ask because I was surprised at you—and at him."

Amber chuckled. "He's a gentleman."

"I believe so."

Her cheeks were burning now, but she had to say it. She gave Lenny a shamefaced grin. "But neither of us wanted him to be."

Lenny laughed. "Well, that's good news on both fronts. That the chemistry's there and that you both have enough sense not to act on it immediately."

"I know, right?"

"So, when are you seeing him again?"

"Tonight."

"Wonderful. And are you going to tell your parents that you've met someone?"

Amber's smile faded. "Not yet."

Lenny gave her a stern look. "You know, I'm half-tempted to tell them that I need you to stay."

Amber's heart leaped in her chest. "Would you? That'd make everything so much easier."

"No. It wouldn't be right, Amber. It'd make life easier, but easier isn't always better. In fact, it rarely ever is. You need to step up. Tell them the truth. Tell them you don't want to go back."

"I don't want to let them down."

Lenny sighed. "You won't. If anything, you're stringing everyone along by leaving the door open. They still hope that you'll go back to him, you know."

"Of course, I know. They'd be happier if I did, wouldn't they?"

Lenny blew out a sigh. "Right now, they would. But only because they don't know the whole story, do they?"

"I didn't want them to worry or be upset. They like Milo. And he's good for the business. Since he's been there, they've been able to step back. They're so much better together now. And that's thanks to him."

"That's a maybe. He took some of the burden off your father. But from what Jade tells me, he landed much of it back on you anyway."

Amber shrugged. "He must have figured it out by now. I've been here for months."

"You're talking yourself in circles. If he's figured it out, then he doesn't need your help anymore. So, you can tell them all that you're not going back. Let them hire someone permanent to do the books. Let them all know that there's no hope of you going back to Milo. That way, they can move on. And more importantly, so can you."

"I know you're right."

"So why not just do it?"

"I should. They said they might come up and visit soon. I should sit down with them when they do. I want to figure out what I could do here first. You've made it clear you don't want me forever."

Lenny chuckled. "I've made it clear I don't need you. If you want to stay, you can have a job. I've been thinking I should hire someone. I'm ready to admit that I've enjoyed taking it easier. I wouldn't mind going part time and bringing someone in full time."

Amber raised an eyebrow. "Do you mean that? Or are you just saying it to make me feel better about staying?"

Lenny laughed. "Unlike you, I've never put feelings above practicalities. Of course, I'd love you to stay. I wouldn't mind if you want to work here. But I don't need you. And I'm not trying to influence your decision. You have to figure it out for yourself, and what I'd love to see you do is decide what you actually want and go after it."

Amber smiled. "I'm trying. I can tell you that what I want right now is for seven o'clock to roll around."

Lenny laughed. "Where's he taking you?"

"We're going to Giuseppe's for dinner."

"Have you ever been out to his place?"

"No."

"You should get him to take you."

"Why's that?"

Lenny laughed. "Apart from the obvious. You should see where he lives. It'll tell you a lot about him. Help you get to know him better."

"What do you mean?"

"You'll see when you go."

~ ~ ~

"Come here, Roscoe."

Roscoe came bounding over to where Austin was sitting on the sofa and stuck his head in his crotch.

He pushed him away with a laugh. "Get out, perv!"

Dallas laughed. "He's not stupid. He can smell the blue balls."

Austin threw a cushion at his brother, but he caught it. "Leave it, D."

Dallas shrugged. "I will. What I don't understand is why you did."

"I've told you. I like her. She likes me. There's no hurry. It's not about just getting her into bed."

"Why not, though? I get that you're not looking for just a quick hookup. But if you're looking for a deep meaningful connection, why not connect—balls deep—from the get-go?"

Austin had to laugh. "Because in my world getting to know a woman is about more than just that. It'll come—in time if it's right."

"And how's that been working out for you? You took your time with Nadia."

Austin made a face. "I was younger and dumber when we got together. Don't give me any shit about her. She came and gave me a mouthful last night."

"She did? How did Amber handle that?"

"She was very understanding." He smiled. "And we didn't have to deal with the full-blown drama. Kenzie cut Nadia off, dragged her away before she could really get started."

Dallas grinned. "I like Kenzie."

Austin gave him a dark look. "She's married."

"I know, but she doesn't strike me as someone—"

"Don't. Okay? I get the impression that you would have been right about her once upon a time when she first came here. But not anymore. She's head over heels in love with Chase, and he's the same with her. In fact, he would have been a good hunting buddy for you before he met Kenzie."

Dallas nodded. "Makes sense—singing in the band would put a guy in a position where he'd have his pick of all the hot chicks."

"Yeah, and he used to make the most of it, but not anymore. He's grown up. You might want to think about trying that."

Dallas laughed. "I have. I am. I'm only teasing you."

"Yeah, right. Are you ever going to tell me why you're really here?"

Dallas shrugged. "I felt like coming home. And … I know I haven't actually said it in words, but I appreciate you letting me stay."

Austin smiled. "No problem. I like having you. Any idea how long you're going to be here?"

Dallas laughed. "You like having me, but you want to know when you'll be rid of me?"

"No. I'm just wondering what's going on with you."

"So am I. If you want to know the truth, I got bored. I felt like I got … lost. I mean, LA's great. And the women and the parties and … everything. But there's no … I dunno. Nothing feels real or genuine."

Austin raised an eyebrow. "And that matters to you?"

Dallas threw the cushion back at him. "Of course, it does. I joke around a lot, but it's only fun. I might be more easy-going than you are, but they raised us with the same values." He blew out a sigh. "You'd laugh if you saw me in the city. Down there they think I'm all stuffy and responsible."

Austin had to laugh. "Damn. I'd hate to see what they're like, then."

"You would. You'd really hate it."

"So, you don't plan to go back?"

Dallas shook his head slowly. "The thought doesn't hold much appeal. But what could I do here?"

Austin sucked in a deep breath. "I know someone who might be looking to hire."

"Who? To do what?"

He smiled, knowing that he might live to regret this. "Me. To lighten my load."

Dallas's eyes grew wide. "You'd hire me?"

He nodded. "We'd have to talk about it first, lay out some ground rules, but yeah. You could study for your license. And in the meantime, you could help in the office, learn the ropes."

Dallas cocked his head to one side. "Why?"

"Why not?"

"I'm serious, A. I want to know why. Just to help me out?"

"No. Because I need some help. Things have really taken off around here over the last few years. And this last year it's gone crazy."

"Dare I even ask just how well you do?"

Austin pursed his lips. "You probably don't want to know."

Dallas grinned. "I do if I'm going to start getting a piece of it."

"Okay. Let's put it this way. Last week I closed on a house, the sale price was in the multiple seven figures."

"Damn!"

"Yeah. And, as the buyer's agent, I'm looking at three percent."

"Double damn! So, you do a couple of those a year and you're laughing."

Austin did laugh at that. "I've already done a couple of those this year, and a bunch more that weren't as expensive, but still." He thought about it for a minute. "Since Christmas, I've done over a dozen sales at more than half a mill each."

Dallas frowned as he did the math. He raised his eyebrows when he figured it out. "And that's just the high-end stuff?"

"Yup."

"Wow. And then you have the whole rental business, too. Property management?"

"That's right. There's the commission on the properties I manage and the rental income from the ones I own."

"I'm not even going to ask how many you own."

Austin was glad. "I'm only telling you so that you know … know that if you want to come in, there's money to be made. And I could use the help."

"Why me, though? I don't know the first thing about real estate. All I know about houses is that you live in them."

Austin smiled. "You're a fast learner. When something sparks your interest, you pick it up in no time. People love you. You'd be great with the clients. And …"

"And what?"

"And on a personal level, I'd love to have you home—and to work together."

"Aww. Are you going to cook for me and take care of me, too?"

"Hell, no. Your first priority would be to find your own place."

Dallas grinned. "I like the idea of it."

Austin's heart sank. He should have led with something other than the money. Dallas could do well for himself, there was no doubt about that. But Austin wanted him to do well for the clients too.

"What do you like most about it?"

"I won't deny that the idea of making a shit ton of money has its appeal. But … I like the idea of working with you. I know I can be a pain in your ass—but that's only when we're fooling around. I wouldn't be like that at work. And even aside from that … I've never thought about it before, but it's a pretty cool business, isn't it? You get to help people find their homes. That's one of the biggest decisions in a person's life. It's a big deal, in every sense."

Austin relaxed. "It is. I thought you might laugh at me, but you get it. It's a big responsibility. But it's really rewarding."

Dallas smiled. "Okay. I'm going to do some research and see if I think I'm a good fit. In the meantime, you have a think. I won't be upset if you decide that it's not a good idea. It's one thing to sit here and kick the idea around. Actually doing it … well, I want you to be sure first."

"Okay. How about we talk about it again next weekend?"

"Sure. Whenever you like." He looked up at the clock on the wall. "But this weekend isn't about work. This weekend is about you and Amber. I'm going to take myself into town tonight—and don't worry. I won't be back."

Austin pursed his lips. He was about to protest that he didn't plan to bring Amber back here, but … He didn't want to rule the possibility out either.

Dallas chuckled. "Go for it. You know you want to."

"Of course, I want to, but I'm not into immediate gratification." He waggled his eyebrows at his brother. "It may come as a surprise to you, but anticipation—the buildup—can be enjoyable, too."

"Hmm. I'll have to take your word for that. But even if you don't want to bring her back here to screw her brains out, you could still bring her, just to hang out—just the two of you."

"I could." Austin liked the idea, but he wasn't sure it'd be wise. He hadn't expected Amber to be so willing last night. If they were alone together here, he didn't know if either of them would be able to hold out.

It turned out that it wasn't a decision he needed to make.

~ ~ ~

Amber blew her nose loudly and went to splash cold water on her face. It was red and blotchy. She looked a mess. She felt a mess, too.

She dried herself quickly when she heard the front door close. "Hey, sis. I'm back. Ally's with me."

That made her eyes fill with tears again. She'd been waiting for Jade to get home, but she'd expected her to be alone. "I'll be right out."

She tried to make herself look presentable, but there was no disguising the fact that she'd been crying.

"Are you okay in there? Do you want a glass of wine?"

"Yes, please. I'll be out in a minute."

She considered putting some mascara on, but that'd probably only make her look worse. There'd be no hiding it from Jade anyway. She opened the door and went to the kitchen.

Ally was sitting at the counter with her back to her. Jade frowned as soon as she saw her.

"Uh-oh. What happened?"

She shrugged. She didn't want to start crying again. She'd only just managed to stop.

Jade came around the counter and Ally turned to look at her.

"What is it, sis? Austin?"

"No!" Crap! She hadn't even thought about that. She couldn't go out with him tonight.

Jade frowned. "What then?"

She could feel her lower lip trembling. "Milo."

"What? What's he done?" Jade's tone was sharp.

"Don't be mad at me." The tears were starting to fall again.

Jade gave her a quick hug. "I'm not mad at you. I'm mad at him. What's he done? How's he upset you?"

"He called." She sniffed.

"And said what?"

"That Mom and Dad really miss me and want me to come home."

"Bastard! He's just messing with your head Amber."

"Too right he is!" She hiccupped back a sob. "He knows how much I love them. He knows I don't want to let them down."

"And he's using it against you to get what he wants."

"I told him that even if I go back, I'm not going back to him."

Jade gave her a dark look. "Yeah, right. He knows, and I'm half inclined to agree with him, that if you go back there, he'll be able to worm his way back in. You have to stay here. Stay away from him."

"I want to stay away from him, but … I can't let them down."

"You're not. For crying out loud, Amber! Don't let him use your sense of duty against you! Why can't you see it? If you'd just tell Mom and Dad the truth—that you're happier here and you don't want to go back—they'd be fine with it. They'd be happy for you. They're only holding out because you haven't told them not to."

Amber stared at her for a long moment. "I don't want to do that to them."

"Why won't you get it through your head? Doing what you want for yourself is not doing anything bad to them. You have to put yourself first. Most people do it naturally, you know."

Amber stared at her. "I don't want to be selfish."

"Ugh!" Jade looked at Ally. "Can you talk any sense into her?"

Ally gave Amber a warm smile. "She's right, you know. You remind me of my mom in a lot of ways. She stayed with my dad far too long because she was so used to putting him—and us—first. Doing what you want isn't selfish. It's how life's supposed to work. The people who love you—your parents—won't have a problem with you doing what makes you happy. The only people who have a problem with it are the ones who really are selfish, the ones who want you to do what they want instead. It sounds like this Milo is one of those." She made a face. "From what Jade's told me, he sounds like my dad. He made my mom miserable for thirty years. Do you really want that for your life?"

Amber shook her head. She'd loved the feeling of freedom she'd had since she and Jade came here—since she'd left Milo. She loved Ally's mom, Audrey. She was awesome, and she was so happy and in love with the new man in her life. She shuddered at the thought of spending thirty years with Milo before she ever got to find happiness like Audrey had with Ted.

"I just don't want to let anyone down."

"You're not—" Jade began, but Ally held up her hand.

"Can I give you a different perspective?"

They both nodded.

"My mom didn't want to let me and Brayden down. She knew she was miserable, but she felt like she had to hold the family together. You know … that we should have our dad in our lives … and we should all be together. All that did was make all of us miserable. He cheated on her for years, then dumped her for someone our age. I grew to hate him and had started to avoid him even before they broke up. Brayden tried to be the peacekeeper—and ended up feeling like a failure because he couldn't bring everyone back together." She blew out a sigh. "My point is that by trying not to let anyone down, Mom inadvertently made things worse for all of us, and dragged out the misery way longer than it needed to last."

"See," said Jade. "It's like I've been telling you. You need to rip off the Band-aid. Tell the folks you're not going back and tell them once and for all that you're never getting back with Milo."

Amber nodded. She could see the sense in everything they were saying. She could see that her sense of duty and responsibility probably was as misguided as they thought. But she didn't feel brave enough to just do it.

Jade patted her arm. "Come on. Have a glass of wine. You need to cheer up. You'll have to get ready soon."

She sniffed. "I'm not sure I want to go."

"What?!"

She blew out a sigh. "How am I supposed to go out with Austin when I'm all confused about Milo and going home? If I have to go back, then there's no point in starting seeing him."

"Jesus, Amber! For someone who's supposed to be so smart, you are the dumbest person I know. You don't have to go back. You just have to go after what you want."

"Well, I don't want to string Austin along, not until I know what I'm doing. I know that much."

"So, you're not going to go tonight?"

She shook her head. She'd been so looking forward to seeing him again, but since she'd talked with Milo, it just didn't feel right. Milo had talked as if she were still his girlfriend. She wasn't, but still … It'd made her realize that until she got her act together and made the commitment to either go back, or never go back, it wouldn't be fair to start anything with Austin.

"You're nuts."

"Maybe. Maybe I just need a bit of time."

"You'd better call him and tell him."

Ally looked at them wide-eyed. "You're serious?" She looked at Jade. "And you're not going to talk her into her going?"

Jade rolled her eyes. "I know there's no point in trying. I'm mad at her. I think she's being totally stupid. But I know her well enough to know that she won't change her mind. So, me yelling at her will only add to the stress and won't solve anything." She gave Amber a grudging smile. "So, after she's called Austin to tell him that she'd not going to see him. We're going to get her drunk."

Amber smiled back. "Thanks. I think I need that."

Ally shook her head in wonder. "I'm not sure I agree with any of this. I think you should call your ex back and tell him to go screw himself. Then call Austin and ask him to come screw you."

Amber chuckled. "And if I were someone else, I'd love to do both of those things. But I'm not. I need to work my way up to them."

Jade poured three glasses of wine and handed one to Amber with a weird look. "Just don't take too much longer about it. Or I might have to step in and help."

"What do you mean?"

Jade shrugged. "I don't even know yet."

# Chapter Seven

Austin looked around at all the cars parked in the square. It seemed like half the town was here. He didn't want to face any of them. Didn't want to hear the questions about how last night had gone. He pulled in and parked next to Colt's truck and cut the engine and sat there for a minute.

He needed to try and look on the bright side. When Amber had called him last night to cancel she'd said—and repeated three times during the course of the conversation—that she did want to see him again. That she wasn't blowing him off, just that she couldn't see him last night.

He didn't think she was a liar. But she was the kind of girl who wouldn't want to hurt anyone's feelings. Was she lying so that she didn't hurt his? If she was, he'd rather she'd just told him the truth. This way, he wanted to believe her, wanted to hope that she would call him like she'd said, but he didn't know if that made him stupid.

He got out of the SUV and plastered a smile on his face. He wished he'd decided to stay home and hide out instead. But that would have meant facing Dallas when he got back, and that was probably worse than this.

He walked across the deck of the Boathouse, thinking that he could probably find himself a table inside and have some lunch alone and unnoticed while most people sat outside in the sunshine to make the most of the beautiful day.

He almost got away with it, too. He was about ready to call for the check when Ben, who owned the resort, spotted him.

"Hey, bud. I haven't seen you in a while. How's it going?"

Austin nodded. "It's going. How about you? How's Charlie?"

The way Ben smiled made Austin wonder what it must feel like to love someone as much as Ben obviously loved his wife. "She's great. We're great. We're taking off next week, going on a mini vacation, just to get a break."

Austin smiled. "That's good. I remember the days when you were here twenty-four-seven, and even suggesting that you should take a break earned me an earful."

Ben chuckled. "So do I. That seems like a different lifetime now. Now, I worry about you working all the hours that you do. You should do something about that."

"I've been thinking about it. You know Dallas is back? Well, I'm thinking about bringing him on board."

Ben raised an eyebrow. "You think he'd do okay?"

"Yeah. He's grown up a lot."

"Then I reckon that'll be awesome—for both of you. But when I said you should do something about working all the time, I meant do the kind of something that involves a woman. Find someone who makes you want to do things other than work."

Austin made a face.

"What?"

If he could tell anyone, it'd be Ben. "I thought I might have."

"Amber?"

He nodded.

"That's great—isn't it? I've been waiting to hear about you and her getting together ever since you and Nadia broke up. I heard you were in here with her on Friday night."

"I was, and I was supposed to see her again last night."

"But you didn't?"

"No."

They both turned at the sound of someone clearing their throat.

Diego gave them a half apologetic smile. "I'm sorry to interrupt. But I can't help myself."

Ben laughed. "I've heard that about you a few times now."

Diego laughed. "I am curious, but perhaps it is better that I don't ask." He turned his gaze on Austin. "I came to check on you, my friend."

Austin smiled. "I'm good, thanks. How are you settling in?"

"I am wonderful, but I do not believe that you are good. You are sad, no?"

How did he even know? Austin blew out a sigh. This was Summer Lake; everyone got to know everything at some point, and usually sooner than you'd expect. "Yeah. I am," he admitted.

Ben raised an eyebrow at him.

"Same thing you were asking about. I was out with Amber on Friday night. I was supposed to see her again last night, but she canceled on me."

Diego frowned. "Why?"

"She said she had some stuff to deal with."

"What stuff?"

"I don't know."

"Is it something to do with her parents and her ex?" asked Ben.

Austin nodded slowly. That would make sense. "Probably."

"What's the story there?" asked Diego.

"I don't really know. It sounds like he was controlling. But he works for her parents, and they like him."

"And he wants her back?" Diego's eyebrows knit together.

"Yeah. She said she's not interested, but she also said she'd have dinner with me last night."

"I think she's the kind of girl who puts other people's needs before her own," said Ben. "I know Lenny worries about her."

"Why?"

"Because she doesn't want her to go home."

Diego grinned at Austin. "Then you must persuade her to stay—help her do what's best for herself."

Austin let out a short laugh. "I'd love to, but how am I supposed to do that?"

"Easy, you want a woman, you just let her know that you want her, that you'd be good for her, and you show her that you'll be good *to* her."

"That's easy for you to say."

"It'll be easy for you to do. If you have a little faith in yourself."

Ben smiled at him. "He's right. Most of us mere mortals get caught up in our own stuff—in our own self-doubt. Diego is living proof that when you believe in yourself, you leave no room for anyone else to doubt you."

"It's true," said Diego with a grin. "You want a woman, you have to believe that you'd be good for her. If she has a reason to not want to be with you, you have to find out what it is. Then you can figure out if it's a valid reason—if you have to accept her choice—or if it's simply something you have to be patient with and help her to work her way past."

Austin met his gaze. "Is that what you did with Izzy?"

He nodded happily. "It is. And I can tell you without any hesitation that not giving up on her was the best decision I ever made."

Ben smiled. "Sounds to me like you have a plan to follow, if you want to."

Austin looked at them both. "I do."

Diego held his gaze. "And you also have the balls to follow it through. Don't doubt yourself."

Austin smiled. "Thanks. I'll do my best."

"Don't just say it, do it, mi amigo."

"I'd like to, but I don't know where to start."

"It is simple." Diego smiled. "Where is she this afternoon?"

"I don't know."

"You have her number, no?"

"I do."

"Then you call her. You ask if you can see her—now."

Austin swallowed. "She said she'd call me."

Diego cocked his head to one side but didn't say anything.

Austin's heart was racing now. He didn't think of himself as the pushy kind. He looked at Ben.

Ben chuckled. "I'm the wrong person to ask. I wasted half my life respecting what I thought Charlie wanted. If I'd had Diego around to tell me to try it his way, we'd probably have been back together years ago."

Diego smiled at him. "Isn't she worth at least trying for? Do you want doubt and fear to be more powerful forces in your life than hope and love?"

Austin frowned. Who said anything about love? He didn't ask the question out loud. He'd guess that they could both hear him think it.

Ben smiled. "Right now, you have hope. You'll never know if love could have been in the cards if you let doubt and fear win."

"Call her." Diego nodded at him.

"Right now?"

They both nodded this time.

He pulled his phone out of his pocket. He didn't want to call her with them both standing there watching him.

Diego grasped Ben's shoulder. "We should go. We've said enough. What you do with our words is your choice."

"Thanks, guys." He watched them walk away then looked down at his phone. Maybe he'd go sit in the SUV and call her from there.

"Are you sure you don't want to come?" asked Jade.

Amber shook her head.

"You might have fun. It'd do you good to get out in the sunshine at least."

"I know. But I don't want to. And besides, you'll have more fun if I don't go. You can have a laugh with Ally and the guys and not have to worry about keeping an eye on me. I'm fine. I think I'm going to read. I might just sit out in the yard."

Jade made a face. "I'm not going to keep harassing you. But you need to snap out of it soon, sis."

"I know. And I'm sorry. I don't mean to be difficult. I just want a little time to work things out. I was doing so well. I really was thinking about staying here. But he got to me with what he said last night—about them needing me."

"They don't! Ugh! I'm not going to argue with you because I'm on the verge of losing my temper. I'm going to go and enjoy the afternoon, even if you refuse to. But I'm telling you, Amber. He's messing with your head—and you're letting him."

She nodded sadly. "The stupid thing is, I know it. I know you're right, but I don't know how to get past the feeling that I'm wrong, bad somehow to want to put myself first."

Jade threw her hands up. "I sure as hell don't know how to help you with that one. I'm going."

"I'll see you later."

Jade closed the apartment door with a bang. It made Amber feel even worse. Her sister was only trying to help her. She went to the fridge and filled a glass with ice before she poured a soda. Maybe she should try to lose herself in a book.

She went to get her phone from the counter when it rang. She froze halfway there. What if it was Milo again? She didn't think she could handle that. It'd be better to let it go to voicemail. She approached cautiously, and her heart leaped into her mouth when she saw Austin's name on the display. She'd half expected that she'd screwed things up between them last night. He'd wanted to know what was wrong. It'd felt like he was on her side—just like it had on Friday night—that they were in it together. But she'd had to remind herself that they weren't. She shouldn't get into anything with him if she was going to leave. And if they *were* going to start seeing each other, she shouldn't start it off by burdening him with her ex troubles.

She stared at the phone so long that it stopped ringing. She blew out a sigh. It seemed she was messing everything up when it came to Austin. Maybe he'd leave her a voicemail?

The message notification didn't beep, but a few moments later, the phone started to ring again. This time she snatched it up when she saw his name.

"Hello?"

"Hi, Amber. It's me, Austin."

"Hi." She couldn't help bouncing up and down on her toes. Just hearing his voice speak those few words brought her smile back.

"Listen …"

Her heart sank. He sounded serious. He was probably going to tell her that he'd changed his mind after she'd messed him around last night—that he didn't want to see her again.

"What are you doing this afternoon?"

She bounced again. "Nothing. Jade's gone out with Ally and Brayden and some other friends. I'm ... well, I'm at home."

"Do you want to get together?"

Her heart raced. Of course, she did. But she shouldn't. She chewed her bottom lip. "I'd like to, but ..." Last night, he'd accepted easily enough that she didn't want to see him. It made her sad, but it was easier that way. She'd said that she'd call him but wasn't sure whether she really would. She hadn't thought he'd call her—hadn't thought he'd make the effort.

"But what?" It seemed that today he was feeling more persistent.

"I'm sorry about last night. I really am. I was looking forward to it. But ... honestly ... Milo called me, and he made me think about going home and ..."

"But you don't want to go back do you? Not home and not to him?"

"No, but ..."

"There don't have to be any buts. How about I come pick you up in half an hour? Roscoe would love to see you again."

She had to smile at that. He was making it easy for her to say yes—and she did want to. "Okay, then."

She could hear the relief in his voice. "Great. I'll see you in half an hour."

As soon as she hung up, she wondered if it had been a mistake. None of her reasons for *not* wanting to see him last night had changed. She smiled. But her reasons for wanting to see him were winning out now. She'd expected him to bow out. She hadn't thought that he'd persist. She ran into the bathroom to check herself over in the mirror. She was okay, but she could maybe put a sundress on instead of her shorts. And she should tie her hair up; it was a mess.

It felt like a lot less than half an hour before the buzzer sounded, and she went to answer it.

"Hey, it's me." His voice sent shivers down her spine.

"Hi. Do you want to come up, or should I come straight down?"

"Come on down. We can get going. I left Roscoe at home."

She smiled to herself. They were going to his place? She liked that idea. "I'll be right there." She ran down the stairs but stopped to compose herself before she opened the front door. She needed to be careful about what she was doing here. She shouldn't get caught up in the excitement of it. That wouldn't be fair to him.

She sucked in a deep breath and let it out slowly before she stepped outside. When she saw him, her next breath caught in her chest. He was gorgeous! He was leaning against his SUV, wearing a denim shirt and shorts. Phew! She wanted to fan herself as a rush of heat hit her.

"Hi." He pushed away from the SUV and came toward her with a big smile on his face.

She smiled back. She couldn't do anything else. "Hi."

He came straight to her and put his hands on her hips as he dropped a kiss on her lips.

Wow! And she thought she'd set them back by telling him she couldn't see him last night. She felt unsteady on her feet.

He didn't let go of her and she rested her hands on his arms—yep, his muscular arms! She looked up into his eyes, and they were doing the gold and green shimmery thing again. She could quite happily get lost in them and forget all about reality for a while.

He smiled, and when he did, she relaxed. It felt like he was her best friend somehow. "I know you said you'd call me, but I didn't want to wait."

"I'm glad."

He slid his arms around her and hugged her to his chest. She couldn't help snuggling against him. He rested his chin on top of her head and she felt him relax, too. "You have no idea how happy I am to hear you say that."

She leaned back to look up at him.

"Last night, I thought you were dumping me before we got started," he explained.

She tightened her arms around his waist. "I don't want to."

His smile faded. "But you're still thinking about it?"

She sighed. "Maybe you should come in, and I should explain. You might want to dump me when you know."

He held her closer. "How about we go to my place, and you can explain? I wasn't kidding; Roscoe wants to see you."

"Okay, then. As long as you know that you might want to bring me straight back home after we talk—and we have to talk."

He didn't answer. He just opened the door for her with a smile that said he didn't plan on bringing her straight home.

# Chapter Eight

Austin was feeling pretty good by the time he pulled off East Shore Road and into his driveway. Amber raised her eyebrows as they waited for the gates to roll back.

He smiled. "I sold so many houses that had these gates, and I think they're cool, so I got myself some, too."

She nodded. "They're very cool. I like it."

As he started up the driveway, it occurred to him for the first time to wonder what she might think of the place. He loved this house. He'd bought it several years back and had spent a couple years remodeling it. It'd been way out of his price range when he bought it—at least it would have been if it were in the shape it was now. But it had stood empty for years since the previous owner had died. It had needed a lot of work, and he'd done it. At first, he'd done the work himself whenever time and money allowed. Then as his business had grown, he'd hired people. He smiled when the SUV emerged from the trees that lined the driveway and the house appeared in the clearing.

"Wow!" She looked shocked.

He didn't know what to say. Dallas had told him that he should make the most of the place—that he should bring women back here to impress them. He was more of the school of thought that if a woman was impressed by his house, she probably wouldn't be impressed with him. Nadia had proved him right about that.

He cut the ignition and turned to look at her. He didn't know what to say, so he waited for her.

Her eyes were wide. "It's lovely!"

"I'm glad you like it."

"Did you grow up here? Is this your family home?"

He had to laugh at that. "No. We lived in town."

"I see."

He didn't know what she thought she saw, but she didn't seem like she was about to explain it.

"Come on. Let's go get Roscoe. He's no doubt scrabbling at the door to get out."

She smiled and followed him to the front door, where Roscoe was indeed bouncing up and down scratching at the door and barking. Austin wondered if he shouldn't have had Amber wait in the car. Roscoe didn't always do well with strangers.

She tapped on the glass pane in the door and called. "Roscoe! Hey, Roscoe, it's me. Do you remember me?"

To Austin's amazement. Roscoe calmed right down. He pressed his paw against the glass and let out a happy-sounding little yip.

She looked up at him and laughed. "I think he might!"

He unlocked the door and opened it with a smile. "He sure does."

Roscoe came out and bounced around him for a few moments before turning his attention to Amber. Of course, he had to stick his nose in her crotch! Her cheeks colored up as she tried to push him away. "Roscoe! I'm happy to see you, too, but we don't know each other that well yet."

Austin couldn't help but laugh at that. "I'm taking notes here. How long will it take before that's an acceptable greeting?"

Her cheeks turned a deeper shade of red as she looked at him, but she laughed.

Luckily, Roscoe wasn't too determined to explore her. He sat down beside her and rested his head against her leg. Austin was thrilled to see it. It'd taken him a good few days to stop growling at Dallas when he came to stay—and he'd known him for years.

"Come on in. Would you like something to drink?"

"I'd love a soda."

He'd wondered if she might want to have a glass of wine with him—or whether offering one might seem like he wanted to get her more relaxed.

He took hold of her hand and led her through to the kitchen. It was probably overkill just to walk that short distance, but he was taking what Diego had said very seriously. He wanted her to know that he wanted to be with her—and that he'd be good to her if he was.

Nadia had always bitched at him that he didn't hold her hand. It was true, he rarely did, but that had been about the way she was, not the way he was. He'd held her hand in the beginning, but to him it was a natural thing to do, because he felt it. Nadia had expected it—as some kind of required demonstration of affection. She didn't just expect it; in the end, she'd demanded it.

Amber looked up at him and he had to wonder why in hell he was thinking about Nadia when she was here. He knew the answer straight away. He was appreciating just how different Amber was.

"Jeez!" She breathed. "This place is …"

"What?" It was important to him to know how she might finish that sentence. That final word, whichever one she chose would tell him a lot about her.

She shook her head. "It's beautiful! Everything about it. I mean, of course, I'm a little bit taken aback that you live in …" She shrugged. "Some kind of rich guy mansion." She gave an embarrassed little laugh. "Sorry. I don't know how to put it. But …" She turned around taking in the entrance they'd just come from, the kitchen which he knew many chefs would kill for and the nook with the breakfast area built into the huge bay window, which overlooked one of the best views in the whole county. "But I can see why. Everything about it is just beautiful. The light, the views, of course all the furniture and everything. My dad would think he'd died and gone to heaven if he saw this kitchen." She looked up at him. "You did it all yourself, didn't you?"

"What makes you think that?"

She smiled. "It's so … welcoming. I mean, normally in a house like this I'd be worried to touch anything—you know? But this feels really … homey, even though it's all so beautiful."

He went to her and closed his arms around her. He hadn't intended this to be a test, but it turned out that it had been— and she'd passed with flying colors. "Thank you. That might be the nicest compliment I've ever had."

She looked up at him. "I'll bet you've heard much more eloquent praise for this place."

"Nope. I don't have people over often."

She frowned but didn't question him.

"Anyway. Let's get that soda."

Amber wandered over to the windows while he fixed their drinks. This place was amazing. And the view of the lake from here was something else. She and Jade had been born here in Summer Lake, but she didn't remember it. Their parents had moved to Bakersfield when they were still tiny. Since they'd come up to help Lenny out, Amber had fallen in love with the place. It was so beautiful, and this view of the lake and surrounding mountains might be the most beautiful she'd seen yet.

Austin came and stood behind her. He rested his hand on her shoulder, making her close her eyes for a moment. If the feel of his hand on just her shoulder had that effect on her, what would it feel like if ... She opened her eyes and turned to smile up at him.

"I want to say you're so lucky to live here, but it isn't luck, is it?"

"It is in some respects. I was one of only a few people who knew it was for sale. I knew the family. It belonged to an old couple, Mr. and Mrs. White. She died years and years ago. He kept the place, refused to leave. And after he died the family couldn't agree what to do with it, so it stood empty for years. When they finally decided they were ready to sell, they came to me to list it. I asked if I could buy it and told them they should get someone else to tell them what they should ask for it. I wanted it all to be above board. But they knew what they wanted to get out of it and chose to save the fees rather than involve another agent."

Amber raised an eyebrow, not sure she understood.

"Normally on the sale of a house, six percent goes to the realtors which the listing agent and the buyer's agent split."

"Oh, okay."

He smiled. "Sorry. You weren't asking how I bought it."

"No, but it's interesting to hear. Was it very run-down—if it'd been empty for years?"

"It was. I'm glad though. I wouldn't have been able to afford it otherwise."

Roscoe chose that moment to come and stick his nose up her skirt. She laughed and pushed him away.

"Roscoe!" Austin gave him a stern look and he peeked his head back out with what Amber could only describe as a grin on his face.

She had to laugh. "Don't look so pleased with yourself. That's rude. I won't be able to come and see you again if you're going to do that."

Austin squatted down and took Roscoe's face between his hands. "Did you hear that, bud? You're about to blow it, for both of us. Can you please behave? I'm trying to make a good impression here."

A rush of warmth filled Amber's chest when they both turned to look up at her. It surprised her that he'd admit that he was trying to make a good impression. She wanted to let him know that he had. She smiled. "Don't worry. I don't think I'd be able to refuse if you asked me to come again. I'd just have to wear jeans or something."

Austin looked pleased. He turned back to Roscoe. "Did you hear that? I don't know about you, but I'm enjoying the dresses, so behave." He got to his feet and smiled down at her. "I already know that I'm going to want to ask you over here again."

She had to stop herself from bouncing on her toes. "I ..." she was about to tell him that she already knew that she wanted to come. But then she remembered, and her smile disappeared.

Austin's did to. He raised an eyebrow and waited.

"I'd love to, but I told you we need to talk. I need to explain about last night."

"You already did. Your ex upset you."

"Yes, but more than that. He made me feel like I need to go home."

"But you don't want to."

"No." She pursed her lips. He wasn't making it easy for her to explain.

He gestured for her to sit on the cushioned bench around the breakfast table and went to get their drinks.

She waited for him to join her. "Jade thinks I'm stupid, and you'll probably agree."

He shook his head. "Nope. I know you're not stupid." He held her gaze for a long moment. "Misguided perhaps, by a sense of duty. But you're definitely not stupid."

She blew out a sigh. "It's not that I want to go back to him."

To her surprise, he smiled and took hold of her hand. "So, stay here and start seeing me instead."

Her heart raced. She hadn't expected him to be so ... she couldn't think of the word ... honest? Assertive? "I'd like to."

His smile grew wider.

"But ..."

He squeezed her hand and shook his head. "There doesn't have to be a but. You already went out with him and you know it's not what you want. I'm asking if you want to go out with me and ..."

He didn't finish the sentence and that made her wonder what he could have said—and find out if he was what she wanted? She looked up into his eyes. She liked that he was showing such strong interest, but she was kind of surprised, too.

He smiled. "Sorry. I know I'm being pushy—and that's not like me. But ... I've wanted to ask you out for a long time. You know that. And now that I have, now that you've said yes, I don't want to give up without a fight. I want you to know how I feel." He gave her an earnest look. "Of course, I respect how you feel. If you were saying you weren't sure about whether you still wanted to be with him then I'd butt out. But you're not."

She shook her head. "I really don't. And you know that I've hoped for this—for you and me to go out—ever since we first met."

He smiled. "So, say you'll give me a shot?"

"I want to. But it doesn't seem right—doesn't seem fair to you—when I don't know if I'm going to crumble and go back home. I wouldn't be going back to him, but I would be going because he manipulated me into it. I'm not dumb. I can see it. I know what he's doing. But I'm the sort of person who has a strong sense of responsibility to my family."

"I know. And I like that about you, even if it is working against me right now." He moved closer and leaned toward her, making her heart beat faster.

He brought his hand up and touched her cheek. "I like everything about you. I appreciate that you don't want to lead me on and then walk away. But you've made me aware of the situation, and it's up to me whether I want to take the risk, right?"

She nodded. She found it hard to drag her eyes away from his lips, knowing that any second now they were going to meet hers. She looked up into his eyes.

"I'm prepared to take the risk. If you'll let me?"

She nodded again, and her eyes fluttered closed as his lips came down on hers. His arm curled around her and pulled her against him. She brought her hands up to his shoulders and clung to them as he kissed her deeply. There was something about his kisses. He wasn't wild or demanding, but he made her squirm in her panties the way he opened her up and his tongue slid inside.

His hand closed around the back of her neck, and she sagged against him, wishing that he was the kind of guy who'd make good on what his kisses suggested.

~ ~ ~

Austin was surprised at himself. He knew that if it weren't for Diego's encouragement, there was no way he would have been so honest with her. He would have waited for her to decide what she wanted and gone along with it. This felt strange, but it felt good. And he could tell by the way she was reacting to him that it felt good to her, too. Not just the kisses, but from the way she kissed him back, those were making her feel good. But more than that, he was being honest about what he wanted. He was still listening to her, but instead of focusing on her doubts, he was focusing on the hope that she wasn't denying what she felt about the two of them.

When he finally lifted his head, he looked down into her eyes. "So, will you go out with me again?"

She nodded, but didn't look as happy about it as he'd like her to. "I will." She sucked in a deep breath. "You know I want to, but I think I need to put one condition on it."

He frowned. "What condition?"

"I'd like to see you—to keep seeing you. But my parents are supposed to come up soon. I don't know when yet. But within the next couple of weeks. So, how about we see each other until they do, on the understanding that I might find that I need to go back with them."

He sucked in a deep breath. He couldn't argue with that. "Okay." He smiled. "That'll give me the chance to persuade you that you'd rather stay here. And when they come, you can tell them that."

"When they come, I'll be able to talk to them without him around. To see if they really do need me."

Austin nodded. He wouldn't want her to let them down if they needed her. No matter what he might want for himself. He understood loyalty to family. He smiled. "Okay then. Now that we have that figured out. How about we get on with just having some fun?"

"I'd like that. What did you have in mind?"

The glint in her eyes let him know that she'd be up for the kind of fun that that kiss had left him longing for, but he couldn't go there. A thought struck him and he couldn't help smiling. He might be crazy—might be cutting off his own nose to spite his face, but not really. "I don't think we should think about *that kind* of fun if you're not going to stay here."

Her mouth fell open and a comical little oh sound fell out.

He chuckled. "I'm not saying I don't want to. But it just doesn't seem right. To me, that's part of a relationship—a real relationship. So, until we know if you're going to stick around for one of those, we should stay away from that."

She searched his face. "You're serious?"

He nodded. He was also wondering if he might be stupid, but he meant what he'd said. He wasn't someone who slept around. He'd only ever slept with girls he'd been in a relationship with. It was just part of who he was.

"Well. Okay then." She didn't look too sure about it.

He raised an eyebrow. "You're good with that?"

She nodded slowly. "If you are."

He couldn't help but chuckle. "I am, but I'll be hoping that your parents come and visit real soon."

She laughed. "Me, too."

It was late by the time he dropped her off back at home. They'd managed to move on from their awkward conversation about whether they were going to see each other again and whether they were going to sleep with each other. He was still surprised at himself about that but it felt like the right thing to do.

When he pulled up in front of her building, he cut the engine and turned to face her. "I had a great time today, Amber."

"I did, too. Thank you—for calling and for not giving up on me after last night."

He smiled. "I was going to. I was going to wait and wonder if you'd call me like you said you would. But ..." He shrugged. "I'm glad I didn't."

"Me, too. Do you want to get together in the week?"

"I'd love to ... when?" He'd been about to ask her, he was thrilled that she'd asked first.

She shrugged. "I'm free whenever." She smiled.

He thought about it. "I have a showing tomorrow evening and ..." He frowned. "I have a meeting on Tuesday after work. That usually runs late. How about Wednesday?"

"That'd be great."

He got the impression that she wasn't thrilled to wait that long. He hadn't done it deliberately, but he was pleased that she was eager. He smiled. "Okay, I guess I'll see you then."

She leaned across the console and landed a peck on his lips. "You will." She smiled. "I feel like the tables have turned somehow. Before you called this afternoon, I was thinking that I shouldn't see you again. Now I can't wait."

He slid his hand into her hair and drew her closer. "I can't either. I wish I could see you sooner. But it's probably better this way."

She raised an eyebrow.

"I've laid it all out on the line for you, Amber. You know what I want. You're the one who still has to decide if I'm worth sticking around for."

She nodded breathlessly. "I already know that you are. I just …" Her eyes dropped to his lips.

He'd heard what he needed to. He didn't have to make her explain it. He lowered his lips to hers and she met him eagerly, kissing him back with a hunger that again made him question the wisdom of saying he didn't want to sleep with her until she knew she was going to stay.

He could have kissed her all night. But he reluctantly broke away. "I should let you go in."

She nodded, and he could tell she didn't want to go. Maybe there was something to what Dallas always said about leaving a woman wanting more. He had no doubt that Amber wanted more from him right now.

He touched her cheek. "Goodnight, Amber."

"Goodnight."

# Chapter Nine

"Where are you guys going?" asked Jade.

"I don't even know! He only texted me this afternoon to say that he'd be here at seven."

Jade smirked. "And it's driving you nuts, right?"

She blew out a sigh. "It is! It shouldn't, but ..." She shrugged. "I suppose it serves me right."

Jade frowned.

"I just mean, I was the one who said I shouldn't see him till I know what I'm doing, and he took me at my word. He made it very plain that he wants us to start seeing each other, but he'll play by my rules until I make my mind up."

"That sounds fair enough to me." Jade chuckled. "If it were anyone else, I'd think he was trying to teach you a lesson."

"What do you mean?"

"The way he's holding back. You're gagging for it, aren't you?"

Amber laughed. "That sounds awful!"

Jade laughed with her. "Only because it's true."

She made a face. "I suppose."

"Well, you can't have it all ways."

"I know. I wish I could just ..."

"Don't bleat to me about it. You're the only one who's stopping you. You could call the folks up right this minute and tell them that you've met someone and that you're not going back. They'd be happy for you once they understood that it's what you want."

"Do you really think so?"

"I know so! Look at the way they are with me. I've always made it clear that I need to do my own thing, and they've never had a problem with it. They accept that's just who I am. The only reason they hold onto you tighter is because you've always let them believe that's what you want."

"I did want. I knew they enjoyed having me around."

"They did. But they don't need you. Why won't you get it through your head? They just want to see you happy. They think—because you've never told them otherwise—that Milo made you happy and that being there—being part of the business—made you happy."

"You really think I created the whole mess?"

"I wouldn't put it that way. You're just too nice. You agree with what you think people want before you know if it's what you want, and then you get yourself stuck and don't know how to get out."

She checked her watch. "He should be here soon."

"I hope you guys have a good time." Jade waggled her eyebrows. "You know, if you called the folks now and told them that you're staying you could tell Austin that you'd made your decision—and I'm sure he'd want to *thank* you."

She had to laugh. "That almost makes me want to do it."

"So, do it! There's no time like the present."

"No, they'll be coming soon. I'd rather sit down with them."

"Have you talked to them this week?"

"No. Have you?"

Jade shook her head. "I might give them a call tonight."

Amber narrowed her eyes at her. "What are you thinking? Why can't you wait till tomorrow and we can call them together?"

Jade smirked. "Don't you worry your pretty little head about it."

"Ugh. I will now. I know that look. You're up to something."

Jade just shrugged and went to look out the window. "He's here!"

Amber grinned. "Okay. I'll see you later."

"I wish you wouldn't."

She made a face. So, did she, but it wasn't going to happen.

~ ~ ~

Austin smiled when he got out of the SUV and the front door opened. Amber bounced out—there was no other word for it—with a big smile on her face.

"Hi!"

"Hi." He'd wanted to call her the last couple of days, wanted to talk to her, see how she was doing, but he'd held back. He was supposed to be giving her some space while she made her mind up if she was going to stay. He'd talked to Dallas about it, and instead of telling him that he should go full on and try to persuade her to stay, he'd told him he was doing the right thing by holding back. Dallas had always had girls running after him, and he did nothing to encourage them. Austin thought of it as the old treat 'em mean and keep 'em keen thing, and his brother didn't deny it.

He didn't want to be mean to Amber, but by the look on her face when she came toward him, she was definitely keen.

He held his arms out to the sides a little way. He wanted to greet her with a hug, but it should be her choice.

She came straight to him and wrapped her arms around his waist. He closed his around her as she stood on tiptoe and landed a kiss on his lips.

He leaned back and looked down into her eyes.

"I missed you."

Wow! She really was keen. He smiled. "I missed you, too. I almost called you."

She gave him a sad smile. "I wish you had. I almost called you, but it felt wrong."

His smile faded. "Wrong? Why?"

"Because I knew you were busy, and I knew I'd see you tonight." She looked up into his eyes. "Honestly, I didn't want you to feel like I was being too much."

He tightened his arms around her. "I wouldn't have. I would have loved it. I'm the one who's respecting your need to take your time."

She smiled. "I feel as though I've had all the time I need." She looked away and when she looked back at him, her face was serious. "Jade told me I should call the folks right now and tell them that I'm staying."

His heart raced in his chest.

She smiled. "I almost did."

He nodded. Almost wasn't the same as doing it. "I hope you'll want to do it soon."

Her smile faded. "I want to do it now, but ..." She sighed. "I was about to say that it's not always about what we want, but maybe it should be."

He landed a peck on her lips. "I can't say anything. I think you know what I'd like to say, but I'm not going to try to influence you into what I want. That'd make me as bad as—" He stopped before he said it, but she knew what he meant.

"No! You're nothing like him. You couldn't be if you tried."

"No?"

"No. You're kind and considerate. You're sweet and …" she shot him a quick glance, "…hot."

He laughed. "Excuse me? Would you mind running that one by me again?"

She smiled through pursed lips. "You're kind and considerate."

"And?"

"Sweet."

"And?"

He sucked in a sharp breath as she pressed herself closer against him and breathed. "Hot." He'd hoped that she might think he was decent looking, but hearing her say he was hot? That made him feel as though he grew a foot taller.

She laughed. "Come on. Don't act surprised. You must know it."

He didn't want to answer that either way. Instead, he shrugged. "Let's get going."

She got in, and when he slid into the driver's seat, she leaned over and pecked his cheek. "Sorry if I embarrassed you."

"No!" He turned to look at her so fast their noses bumped. "You didn't embarrass me. Honestly? You made my day."

"Seriously? I bet you hear that all the time."

He knew he wasn't bad looking; there were a few girls in town who'd made it plain that they liked him, but the way he looked wasn't high on his priority list. He shrugged. "Not *all* the time …"

She laughed. "I knew it."

"That's not the point, though. I don't have any interest in how other people see me. It's none of my business, really. But knowing that you do—that you like me that way …"

She nodded her head vigorously. "I do. I thought you knew that. Right from that first day we met, I thought you were hot."

"Just so you know, I thought you were, too."

She smiled.

"And I think you're even hotter now."

"What changed?"

He smiled. "Now I know you and know that you're as beautiful on the inside as you are on the outside. That counts for a lot in my world."

"Aww." She reached up to touch his cheek. "You're awesome, Austin. How could I even think about going home?"

He cupped her face between his hands and looked deep into her eyes. "I'm hoping you won't be able to."

Amber was surprised, but very pleasantly so, that he didn't slow down when they got to town. She'd thought maybe they were going to Giuseppe's for dinner. Apparently, not. He drove past the square at the resort, too. Not the Boathouse, then.

She glanced over at him. "Where are we going?"

"Oh! Sorry. I didn't even think to ask. My place—if you want to."

Her tummy flipped over. Oh, she wanted to! Her smile faded. But they'd already talked about that. He'd told her that wouldn't be happening until—or unless—she decided that she wanted to stay. She admired that about him. She knew a lot of guys would be more interested in a quick physical fling with a girl who'd be gone soon. Austin wasn't one of them. He didn't work that way.

He glanced over at her. "Is that okay?"

She decided she might as well be honest with him. "It is, but it might be hard."

"How so?"

She felt her cheeks heat up. She wasn't one to talk about sex much. She didn't think she'd ever talked about it with a guy she wanted to do it with. But she felt so comfortable with Austin—she felt safe. And apart from that, she wanted him to know what he did to her.

"It might be hard to keep my hands to myself."

He chuckled, and the sound of it made her press her thighs together. How could a chuckle be so sexy?

"Laugh all you like. You've been warned."

His smile was even sexier than his chuckle when he glanced at her. "Just so we're clear. It won't be any easier for me to keep my hands off you. But I'm a man of my word. That's part of a bigger picture to me. I don't want to go there if we're not going to … go there."

A rush of warmth settled in her chest. He was amazing!

When they got to the house, he took her hand and led her up the steps to the front door. She smiled when she saw Roscoe bouncing up and down behind it. He came bounding out and ran a few circles around Austin before coming to her and sticking his head up her skirt.

"Roscoe!" They both exclaimed as she pushed him away.

"I'm pleased to see you, too, but you really shouldn't."

Austin pushed him away and gave her a mischievous smile. "We're not allowed in there, buddy."

All the muscles in her stomach and lower tightened at the thought of him sticking his head up her skirt—and how his tongue might feel on her skin. She narrowed her eyes at him. "You're the only one who's said that."

He straightened up and came to her. He put his hands on her hips and pulled her closer. The way her body responded to him, he could lay her down right here on the floor in the hallway, if he wanted to.

He kept hold of her hips as he pressed himself against her. He was so hard it made her ache for him. She clung to his shoulders as he covered her mouth with his. She loved his kisses. This time was more urgent. His lips crushed hers, and the way his tongue thrust inside her mouth made her want to feel another part of him thrust inside her.

When he lifted his head, they were both panting. He held her gaze for a long moment. "That was just so you know."

She sagged against him. "What? So I know what I'm missing?"

He chuckled. "I meant so that you know I want to—I want you. But I respect you, and I'll wait."

She let out a big sigh. "I really don't want to wait."

He smiled. "Then, do what you need to do and …."

He left the words dangling, and her lust-addled brain wanted to finish the sentence in a dozen dirty ways.

~ ~ ~

Austin slung his arm around her shoulders as they walked up the path that led away from the pool. They'd eaten a picnic dinner out on the back deck. He enjoyed her company. They'd talked and laughed a lot while they ate. She was bright and funny. She seemed to come out of herself more when it was just the two of them like this.

She looked up at him with a sassy smile. "Please tell me that you're taking me into the woods to have your way with me?"

He laughed. "I'd love to, but no. I want you to see the view from up here."

She looked back over her shoulder. "It looks pretty amazing from here."

"It is. But it gets even better."

They walked on in silence. This last part of the path was steep, but the view would be worth it. They emerged from the trees into a clearing. Amber stopped to catch her breath. She looked up, and her eyes widened.

"Is that what I think it is?"

He grinned. "If you think it's a tree house, then yes, it is."

"Wow! That's amazing! Can we go up?"

"I was hoping so."

He let her climb the ladder ahead of him and did his best not to look up her skirt. He kind of envied Roscoe that he could stick his head in there and get away with it. When she reached the top, he went up after her.

"Oh, my goodness! You weren't kidding, were you? This is amazing."

He leaned on the rail beside her and looked out at the view. They could see the whole lake from here. The house wasn't too far off the road, but the land rose sharply, and this was one of the highest points around without going up into the foothills.

"Isn't it beautiful?"

"Beautiful is far too small a word. You can see where the river flows into the lake and all the way to where it flows out again. The mountains." She pointed. "You can even see town."

He nodded, thrilled that she so was so impressed with it. He'd brought Nadia up here once, but she didn't get it. She didn't understand why a grown man would want a treehouse. And she'd told him in no uncertain terms that when they had children it would have to go. It was a safety hazard. He shuddered at the memory.

"Are you okay?"

He smiled. "I'm great. I'm glad you like it."

"I don't just like it. I love it." She looked behind her at the doorway. "Can we go in?"

He grinned. "Please do."

"Oh, wow!"

The inside of the treehouse was something he'd spent a lot of time on. He'd wanted to make sure that those views could be seen from in here. But he also wanted it to be a comfortable place to hang out and read a book and relax. He'd set windows down low so that when he lay on the bench, he could still see the lake and the mountains.

Amber went and sat down. He was glad that he'd left the foam mattress on the bench. He wanted her to be comfortable.

"I love it. I'd spend my Sunday afternoons out here with a book. Do you do that?"

He nodded. He loved that she got it—that she saw it the same way he did. He sat down and put his arm around her shoulders. "It's a good place."

Her eyes shone when she looked up at him. He felt the change in her, and his body responded. She was no longer thinking about lying here reading a book. Neither was he.

Her fingers slid up into his hair, sending shivers down his back, and making him shift uncomfortably in his pants. She pulled him down until his lips met hers. They were full and soft. Her kisses tasted sweet.

She moaned into his mouth when he curled his arm around her and crushed her to his chest. He needed to be careful. It'd be too easy to get carried away. He couldn't help it. He leaned forward farther, making her lean back. She clung to his shoulders as he leaned farther still until he gently lowered her back onto the mattress.

He shouldn't; he knew it. But just for a moment … He lay down beside her, and it was his turn to moan when she pressed her hips against his. She slid her hands under the hem of his T-shirt. The feel of her warm fingers moving up over his chest made him ache to be inside her.

He couldn't help it. He ran his hand up the back of her leg until he found her full round ass. She gasped and rocked against him. It'd be so easy to …

She sat bolt upright at the sound of barking. "Roscoe?"

Austin sat up and blew a sigh at the ceiling. He'd left him in the house because he didn't want him wandering off while they climbed up here.

He went and opened the door and Roscoe barked happily up at him. He jumped around in circles as if he thought he might somehow be able to jump high enough to reach them.

"Hold on, buddy. We'll be right down." He looked back at Amber.

She was straightening her dress and gave him a rueful smile. "Did you ask him to protect you?"

"From what?"

She laughed. "Did you tell him to make sure that you didn't give in to me?"

He had to laugh. "No. I can't even say I'm entirely glad that he showed up."

She met his gaze. She looked more serious now. "I can say that I wish he hadn't."

Austin felt as though bolts of lightning shot through his veins. He was supposed to be resisting her, but she was irresistible.

"But he's here now." She gave him a rueful smile. "We'd better get down there to him. He'll do himself an injury if he keeps jumping around like that."

# Chapter Ten

Lenny came to stand beside Amber at the counter. "Have you made your mind up?"

Amber smiled at her. "Yes. I think I have."

"Good. And do you want to stay on here with me?"

"What about Jade?"

"Jade will do her own thing either way. She wouldn't want a permanent job, and I wouldn't want to give her one."

Amber frowned.

"Don't look like that. She's more realistic, just like me. She's not going to stay here forever. She's having fun at the moment. She's hit it off with Ally, hasn't she?"

"She has. They're getting really close."

"And you don't mind that?"

Amber had to laugh. "Of course not. We've always been close. We always will be, but we don't normally live in each other's pockets. Living together here has been fun. It's done us both good, and we've loved it. But this is the first time we've lived together since we left home. You know what she's like.

She's been gone different places, working different jobs. Traveling. We're pretty much opposites when you think about it."

"I know you are, but I didn't know if you depended on her."

"No! I guess it might have seemed that way since we've been here. I wasn't in a great place when we came—you know, after breaking up with Milo and everything."

"And you're certain that's over?"

"Oh, my gosh, yes!"

"So, are you going to tell your folks that you're staying?"

She nodded. "I should."

Lenny frowned. "I know you should—are you going to?"

"Yeah."

"Okay. Well, if you want it, I'll be happy to tell them the job here is yours."

"Thanks, Grandma."

Lenny made a face.

"I know you think it makes you sound old. But to me it's a term of endearment."

Lenny's expression softened. "Okay, but just don't say it while there's anyone around." She jerked her chin toward the door where a guy was just coming in.

Amber waggled her eyebrows and spoke in a whisper. "What, you don't want him to know that you're a grandma?"

Lenny laughed. "He might look old to you, but I'm probably old enough to be his mother." She winked. "I do have some vanity left, though." She smiled at the man.

He smiled back as he came to the counter. "Good afternoon, ladies."

"Good afternoon."

Amber couldn't help smiling. He was older, in his fifties, she'd guess, but there was something about him. He was sexy.

"What can we do for you?" asked Lenny.

The man smiled. "Stamps, please. Ten of them."

Once he'd gone Lenny smiled at her. "Do you want to knock off early? You're seeing Austin tonight, aren't you?"

"I am, but I'll stay and close up with you. He's coming for me at seven, and I'll only sit there wishing the time away if I go now."

Lenny laughed. "He's a catch, you know."

Amber frowned. "What do you mean?"

"Exactly what I say. He's a good man. He's done very well for himself. Well, you know, you've been to his place."

She nodded.

"What? What did I say wrong?"

"Nothing. You just reminded me. That's what Mom and Dad used to say about Milo. On paper, he was a catch, as you put it. But those things aren't important to me. You know what Dad's like; it's all about money." She made a face. "I feel disloyal even saying it, but fast food?" she shook her head. "If I wanted to make a fortune, I'd have to find something that meant more than that."

Lenny laughed. "It seems like the sense in our family skipped a generation. Your father was always that way. Even when he was a boy. Anything for a buck." Her laughter faded. "He's my own son, but I was glad when he moved away from here."

Amber nodded. She didn't know what to say. She knew her dad wasn't close with Lenny, but she'd never heard her say something like that before.

She gave Amber a sad smile. "Sorry. That was probably too much. It's just, well, I was always afraid that you girls would turn out like him. That you'd be all about the material things. It's been so good to have you here and get to know you properly."

Amber went to her and wrapped her in a hug. "It's been so good to come here and get to know you properly. I wish you'd been in our lives more before."

Lenny hugged her back and then stepped away. "I do, too, but you're here now, and that's all that matters. That and the fact that you're going to stay. And you're certain about it?"

"I am." She wasn't looking forward to telling her parents, but she was looking forward to having that behind her.

"Good, because I talked to them earlier. They want to come next weekend."

Amber stared at her.

"Don't look at me like that. It's a good thing. The sooner they come, the sooner you can tell them. You can put that life behind you and get started on the one you're going to have here."

~ ~ ~

"Are you out tonight?" Austin asked Dallas.

"Yeah. I think I'm going to stop into the Boathouse. Is that where you're taking her?"

"It is. I don't know how long we'll stay—"

Dallas grinned. "Are you going to bring her back here afterward?"

Austin made a face. "Probably not."

"Hmm, that's better than the outright no I expected."

"I'm not a freaking monk, D. I'd love nothing more than to bring her back here. But I'm trying to wait."

Dallas nodded. "I know. I'm only yanking your chain. But you surprise me. You're crumbling sooner than I expected you to. You like her a lot, don't you?"

"Yeah. I do."

"And you think she's going to stay here?"

He nodded.

"Then, in that case, do you have a place you want to rent to me?"

Austin frowned. "I meant I hope that she's going to stay here in Summer Lake, not here at the house."

Dallas laughed. "I know, dumbass. But if she stays in town, and you two get together, she's going to start staying here at the house, too. You don't need me getting in the way."

"Perhaps you should wait a while. I'm not a hundred percent sure that she won't change her mind yet."

"Either way, I've been thinking about what you said—about me working for you?"

"Yeah?"

"Yeah. If you mean it. I'd like to. But if I do, I think I should get my own place. I only meant to crash with you for a little while anyway. And if we're going to be working together, you're not going to want me in your hair at home, too."

Austin smiled. "I guess you're right. Go on the website, see which places are available, see what you like the look of."

Dallas grinned. "Just like that?"

"Yeah. Just like that."

"Do I get an employee discount on the rent?"

Austin had to laugh. "Sure. You can have the first month free if you need it."

Dallas frowned. "How would that work? I don't want you paying out of pocket for me, and the owners are going to want to get paid."

"So, pick one of my places."

"How many do you have?"

Austin smiled. "Take a look at the website—the business portal, not the public site. You'll see."

"You're not going to tell me?"

"Nope. I'm going to take a shower and get ready to go see Amber."

He was just finishing getting dressed when his cell phone rang. He smiled when he saw Colt's name on the display.

"Hey, bud. What's up?"

"Nothing's up. I wanted to know if you're going to be out tonight—out with the rest of us? Are you going to bring Amber? Or are you doing something just the two of you?"

He smiled. "We're going to come out."

Colt laughed. "Come out as a couple?"

"Yeah. If we're going to start seeing each other, then we need to face the gang at some point."

"Is it still an if? If you're going to start seeing each other? I thought you already were."

"We have been, but she's been figuring out if she's going to stay. So, there was no point getting into anything if she wasn't."

"But she's decided she is?"

"I think so." He'd talked on the phone with her last night and she'd told him that she'd made her mind up. He hoped that she was going to stick to it when she saw her parents. In his mind, he couldn't take anything for granted until she'd told them that she wasn't going home.

"I hope so. What's her problem?"

He sighed. "I'll tell you later. Is everyone going?"

"Yep. All the usual suspects, plus a few more. I was talking to Dan the other day. You know how he's set up this cybersecurity team?"

"Yeah."

"Well, he already has Brayden working for him and a couple others. It sounds like they're going to come out. And I think you can expect a call from him soon, too. He said he wants to set up some kind of corporate housing deal. You know, rent a couple of places from you where he can put his guys while they find their feet."

"Awesome." Austin liked Dan. He'd be happy to set him up with whatever he needed.

"Sorry. The point of all that was that some of the new guys might be out tonight, too."

"Great. Well, I guess I'll see you there. What's Sophie doing?"

Colt laughed. "She's sleeping over at her friend's house tonight. And Cassie's fretting like crazy. So, do me a favor and don't mention Sophie when you see her. You'll only set her off again."

Austin smiled. "Okay. I won't."

It was just before seven when he pulled up outside Amber's place. He smiled when the front door opened. But it wasn't her who came out; it was her sister, Jade. He made to get out, but she shook her head and came to the passenger door and got in.

"Hey."

She smiled. "Don't look so scared. I'm not here to warn you off. I'm here to help you out."

Austin had to smile. She was different from Amber. "That's a relief. What's going on?"

"Nothing new. From what she's told me, you know the deal with her feeling like she should go home."

He nodded. "Yeah. She's told me how she feels about your folks—and about Milo."

Jade made a face. "He's an asshole."

"I've never met the guy, so I shouldn't judge, but I'm inclined to agree with you."

"Good. At least that way you'll be prepared."

"For what?"

She shrugged. "For anything he throws at you. He's holding out for her to go back, and when he realizes that she isn't going, I don't think he'll go down without a fight."

Austin nodded. He didn't know what to say to that.

Jade gave him a long appraising look. "I know it's hardly fair to land you in the middle of it. You've only gone out with each other a couple of times. I wouldn't blame you if you decided it's not worth it."

"No. I know we've only been out a few times. But you know I've liked her ever since you guys first came here. I want to see what can happen between us." He gave her a grim smile. "I'm not some pussy who's going to scare off easily, if that's what this is about?" He raised an eyebrow at her.

She chuckled. "Sorry, you got me. I did want to see where you stand, and I know it's none of my business really. But she's my little sister."

Austin smiled. "I know. And I don't mind. I'm glad you're looking out for her. I want to look out for her, too. But at the same time, she's not some little weakling. She'll make her own decisions."

Jade nodded. "I know. I just wanted to warn you that when I talked to my folks the other night, they still think that she'll go back. I tried explaining to them that I don't think she will, but they didn't take any notice of me. They think that I'm trying to make her go out in the world and do things my way." She let out a short laugh. "They refuse to see that they've made her withdraw from the world and do things their way."

"Withdraw from the world? How?"

Jade shrugged. "They live in a little bubble. All they care about is money and what it can buy." She made a face. "Sorry, that sounds horrible. They're decent people, in their own way. But … I guess what you need to know, is that they think she'd be better off there because she can do her job—which comes easily to her—and have the big wedding and a couple of kids and live in a McMansion and drive a … a …" she laughed. "I don't know, whatever expensive car soccer moms drive these days. You get the idea."

"I think so." It sounded to Austin as though Jade's values were very much at odds with her parents. From what he knew of her so far, Amber's were, too. "So, just so we're clear. What are you telling me?"

She gave him a rueful smile. "I'm not sure I even know. You seem like a good guy. You guys have liked each other from the get-go. I'd like to see you get together, but you're going to have an uphill battle—with Milo, or at least the way he messes with her head. And maybe with my folks, too. They're going to come up here soon. And I'd guess that they'll want to meet you if Amber tells them about you."

"If? You think she might not?"

Jade shrugged. "I don't know what to think." She looked up at the apartment. "I should probably get back up there and send her out." She smiled at him. "I'm rooting for you. I wanted you to know that. And if I can help, I will."

Austin watched her open the door. "Should I come up with you?"

"No. I'll send her down."

"Where did you go?" asked Amber.

"I just took the garbage down." Jade smiled. "And I'll bet you can guess who's down there already."

Amber's heart skipped a beat. "He's here?"

"Yep. And looking like …" She laughed. "I really shouldn't comment on how hot my sister's boyfriend is should I? Let's just say you snagged yourself a hottie."

Amber smiled. "I think so. I didn't realize you did, too."

Jade laughed. "Don't worry, I'm not pining after your man. I appreciate male beauty. You know that."

"He is dreamy, isn't he?"

Jade laughed. "He sure is. After Milo—in fact, even before Milo—I didn't think you had great taste in men—even in just the looks department. Austin's not just an upgrade; he's a whole different league."

Amber nodded happily. "I think so."

"So, stop standing around here swooning over him and get your ass down there. If I were you, I'd be taking him to bed instead of taking him to the Boathouse."

"I'd love to. But he won't do that until I've told the folks that I'm staying here."

Jade frowned.

"He's not trying to make me tell them or anything. He just doesn't want things to get physical if it's not going to last."

"Wow! Most guys I know would have that the other way round. They'd sleep with you till you said that you were staying and then they'd lose interest."

Amber smiled happily. "He's not like most guys, though. He's special."

"He's starting to sound that way. Go on. Go see him. I'll see you at the Boathouse."

# Chapter Eleven

Austin slung his arm around Amber's shoulders as they walked across the square to the Boathouse. When she'd come out of the house, he'd had second thoughts about bringing her to see the gang tonight. He wanted nothing more than to take her back to his place—and to bed.

She was wearing one of those strappy dresses that she seemed to favor. This one had a flowery pattern, and more importantly, it dipped a little lower in the front and clung a little tighter in the back than the others he'd seen her wear. As far as he was concerned, she always looked gorgeous. She was his idea of perfect—not too tall, not too short, and rounded in all the right places. Tonight's dress just showed everything off a little more than usual.

He was already debating with himself whether he could back-track on his insistence that they shouldn't sleep together until she'd told her parents that she was staying here.

She looked up at him and smiled. "Are you okay?"

"I'm great." He stopped walking. "I'm just thinking how lucky I am."

She laughed. "I feel like the lucky one."

He slid his arms around her waist and drew her closer as he dropped a kiss on her lips. "Are you sure you're going to stay?" He was ready to give in when she pressed herself against him.

"I am. I'm going to tell them when they come."

Austin held her gaze for a long moment. He was so tempted to ask if she wanted to go home with him instead of going into the Boathouse. He didn't want to wait another week. And she said she was sure …

The door to the bar flew open, and Jade came hurrying out to meet them.

"Hey, sis." Amber's smile faded. "What's wrong?"

Austin's heart started to pound in his chest. He didn't know why, but the look on Jade's face filled him with foreboding.

"You're going to kill me!" said Jade.

She looked up at Austin. "You too."

"Why?" They both asked at once.

"I screwed up. Big time."

Austin could feel Amber start to tremble, and he pulled her closer into his side.

"What did you do?" Amber's voice sounded shaky.

"I'm sorry. I … Milo called me."

"And?"

Austin's heart was thundering in his ears now.

Jade shot him a worried look. "He was trying to convince me that he'd be good to you if you went back. He wanted me to help talk you into it. Pft! Can you believe that?"

"No. But tell me what you did."

Jade dropped her gaze and then looked first at Amber, then at Austin and back again. She blew out a sigh. "I told him you'd met someone else."

Amber smiled at Austin. "There's nothing wrong with that. I have."

Austin knew there was more to come. From the look on Jade's face, it wasn't anything good.

"I kind of told him that you'd done more than met someone."

Austin didn't get it. Amber didn't either.

"More like what?"

"I'm sorry, sis. He told me that he'd asked Dad if he could ask you to marry him …so, I told him that he couldn't because you were already engaged."

Austin's breath caught somewhere in his chest.

"You what?" asked Amber.

"Yeah. Sorry." She shot Austin an apologetic look, and he realized he must look horrified. He didn't feel it—not horrified. Shocked, yeah, but the thought of being engaged to Amber didn't sound horrific, which surprised him. That was exactly the word he'd used to describe how he felt when he'd told Colt that Nadia thought it was time they got engaged.

"He just pissed me off. He was talking like it was a foregone conclusion that he'd be able to talk you into going back to him. As though marrying him was going to be the best thing for you, and you were just a dumb little woman who was taking her time to figure it out." She shrugged. "I'm sorry."

Amber nodded slowly. "It's not that bad, really, is it?" She looked at Austin. "It's not like he's here or ever going to come here. He doesn't know you …"

"Err …" They both looked at Jade who was looking even more uncomfortable. "There's more."

Austin's heart sank.

"I only talked to him after you guys left the apartment. He wasn't happy. As you can imagine. And I got off the phone as quick as I could. I wanted to tell you what I'd done." She pursed her lips. "On the way over here … Dad called me."

"Oh, shit!" Amber had turned white.

Jade nodded. "Yeah. Sorry. At least he called me and not you."

"I take it Milo had told him?"

"Yup."

"What did he say?"

"That they'll be here next weekend."

Amber blew out a sigh and shook her head sadly. "They were coming anyway. They'd already told Lenny that."

Jade touched her sister's arm. "I'm sorry."

Amber let out a short laugh. "So, you should be." She looked up at Austin. "I'm sorry."

He hugged her into his side. "You haven't done anything wrong." He gave Jade a pointed look. He didn't need to say anything. She knew what he meant.

"I'll have to call them," said Amber. She shook her head. "What am I supposed to say though? I don't want to just outright tell them that you made it up."

"I was thinking about that …"

Austin didn't like the idea of Amber lying to her parents to cover up the fact that Jade had.

"What if you guys went along with it?" said Jade.

Austin frowned. "What do you mean?"

"No!" Amber shook her head adamantly. "I'm not going to lie to them, Jade, and I'm not going to put Austin in that position either."

Jade shrugged. "If that's how you feel, I'll explain it all to them. I don't mind them knowing that I lied. But think about it." She met Austin's gaze for a moment, then looked back at Amber. "What harm would it do? It'd get Milo off your back once and for all. It'd convince Mom and Dad that you have good reason to stay here. Once they meet Austin, they wouldn't have any worries about you … It could work out well all around."

"No." Amber sounded less adamant this time. "No. It's not right to lie." She looked up at him. "I wouldn't ask you to lie."

He was relieved about that, but he could understand Jade's logic. It did sound like … no. He shouldn't even be thinking about it. If he and Amber were going to start seeing each other—if they were going to get serious—he didn't want to start out on the wrong foot with her parents.

Amber's cell phone rang in her purse, and she looked at them with wide eyes. "What do I do?"

"Let it go to voicemail," said Jade. "You need to figure out what you want to say first."

Austin tightened his arm around her shoulders and gave her an encouraging smile. "You might want to look who it is."

She let out a nervous laugh. "Oh. Yeah. Right."

She pursed her lips when she looked at the screen. "It's Lenny. I bet they've called her."

"Shit!" Jade blew out a sigh. "She's going to kill me."

"If she wanted to do that, don't you think she'd have called you?"

Jade's phone started to ring as soon as Amber's stopped. She gave them a wry smile. "I have to talk to her." She walked away. "Hi, Lenny. Before you say anything, can I explain?"

Austin didn't know what to make of any of this. Amber looked up at him with a sad smile. "I'm so sorry. If you want to go—if you want to avoid this mess altogether—I understand."

"No!" He dropped a kiss on her lips. "It is a mess, but I want to help you sort it out, if you'd like me to."

She smiled gratefully. "Thanks."

Jade was coming back to them, still talking on her phone. "Yeah. He's here, too." To Austin's surprise, she handed him her phone. "She wants to talk to you."

"Hi, Lenny."

"Hello, Austin. I'll bet you're wondering what you've landed in the middle of."

"A little bit."

"Well, I can tell you. You've landed in a shitstorm, and if you want to walk away, I wouldn't blame you."

"I don't."

He could hear the smile in her voice when she spoke again. "I had a feeling you might say that. You like her a lot, don't you?" Austin glanced at Amber. It felt strange to admit that he did when she was standing right there.

"You don't need to tell me. But if you do, why don't you go along with this?"

"Why?"

"Because it'd help her out. It'd finally set her free from what she sees as her obligations at home, and it'd clear the way for you and her to have a shot."

"I thought it was clear."

"So did I. It almost was. But if Milo's telling her folks that he wants to marry her ..."

Austin glanced at her. "Then what?"

"Then they're going to put pressure on her to go back. I'm pissed at Jade, but I understand why she did what she did. I know it's not in your nature to lie and deceive people. But you might want to think about this one before you make your mind up."

"Okay."

Lenny blew out a sigh. "Is Amber okay?"

He glanced at her again. "I think so."

"Okay. I'll butt out. Tell her to call me, but I don't mind waiting until after the two of you talk."

"Will do."

"Thanks. And give me back to Jade."

Austin handed the phone back.

Amber came to him with a worried look on her face. "What did she say?"

"That I should consider going along with it"

Amber looked shocked. "She did? Why?"

"Because it'd help you out."

"No. I can sort this out for myself. Jade can sort it out by just telling the truth."

He nodded. He knew she was right, but the more he thought about it, the less of a problem he had with going along with it, if she wanted him to. "When are they coming?"

"Saturday morning. They don't like to be away too long. To them, a weekend away means leaving Saturday morning and getting home Sunday night."

He nodded. If he did go along with it, it wouldn't have to be for long then.

She held his gaze for a long moment then shook her head. "No. Austin. It's not right. It's kind of you to want to help me out, but Jade created the problem. She can solve it, too."

She scowled at her sister when she came back.

"What did Lenny have to say?"

Jade chuckled. "She bitched me out, of course. But then she admitted that it might all work out okay."

"No! She wouldn't go along with it?!"

Jade smiled. "She wants you to call her."

Austin nodded. "She told me that, too."

~ ~ ~

Amber shook her head. She didn't know what to do. She should know what to do. She should call her parents straight away and tell them. But she couldn't make herself do it. She loved them. She'd always done her best to do right by them. She helped in the business because she knew it was the most important thing in the world to them—even if she didn't get why it was. Well, that wasn't true. She knew it was important because it made them so much money. What she didn't get was why money was more important to them than anything else.

"Are you going to come in so I can buy you both a drink?" asked Jade. "It's the least I can do."

Amber looked up at Austin. She felt as though their evening was ruined now.

He smiled at her. "Yeah. Come on. We can have one, and then if you want to go home, I can drive still."

She looked at her sister. "Should I just call them and tell them the truth?"

"No! If that's what you want. I'll tell them. It's all on me. You should text Lenny and tell her you're going to call her when you figure it out, and then turn your phone off. I told Dad that you were out with Austin tonight, so you might not see his call if he tried you."

Amber blew out a big sigh. "I don't know what to do."

"I'm sorry. I know I shouldn't have told him that. But I didn't think. I just got mad."

"I know. I know you meant well. I just don't know what to do with it. I should tell them the truth."

"You know what'll happen if you do though. That'll open the door for Milo again."

"It won't! Why won't anyone believe me that I'm done with him?" She shot a glance at Austin. She didn't want him thinking that there was any possibility that she might actually want to get back with Milo.

To her surprise, he smiled. "I think I know why. It's because you're such a sweet-natured person, and everyone can see it. He thinks he can use it against you to get what he wants. Your parents don't know how you really feel because you're so sweet you don't want to upset them."

She couldn't help smiling back at him. At least, he understood her.

Jade laughed. "I think I'm going to take back my offer of buying you a drink. You two should get out of here. Go off by yourselves and figure out what you want to do."

"You're not getting off the hook that easily."

Jade met her gaze. "I'm not trying to. For me, I'd rather you stayed here and included me in the conversation, but I feel like I'm intruding on the two of you."

Amber looked up at Austin, and he nodded. "I like that idea better."

Wow. She'd half expected him to want out of the situation completely. "Okay."

Jade touched her arm. "I'm so sorry. Call me if you figure out what you want me to do. And don't forget to talk to Lenny." She looked at Austin. "Sorry."

"It's okay."

Amber watched her disappear back into the Boathouse, then looked up at Austin. "Where do you want to go?"

"We could pick up a pizza from Giuseppe's and take it back to my place."

"Okay."

# Chapter Twelve

Amber was surprised to see a Jeep in the driveway when they got to Austin's place.

"That's Dallas. I'm surprised he's still here. He's going to the Boathouse tonight. I thought we'd see him there."

He parked next to the Jeep, and Dallas came out the front door. He looked puzzled as he trotted down the steps with Roscoe on his heels.

He smirked at Austin when he reached them. "Did you change your mind?"

Amber didn't miss the evil look Austin shot him. "We had a bit of a change of plan."

Dallas nodded. "So, I see. I'll be on my way." He grinned at Amber. "It's good to see you again."

"You too."

He gave Austin a meaningful look. "I'll see you tomorrow."

"Okay." They watched him drive away before Austin turned to her. "Come on, let's eat. And I don't know about you, but I'm ready for a drink."

She nodded. She wasn't a big drinker, but she could use one tonight.

They sat at the breakfast table to eat the pizza. As soon as they sat down, Roscoe came and stuck his nose up Amber's skirt. She couldn't help but laugh as she pushed him away. "I've told you; you're not supposed to do that."

Austin rolled his eyes. "I'm sorry. He seems to be pretty taken with you."

She smiled. "I like him, too. But …"

Austin chuckled. "Just because you like him doesn't mean he gets free rein to perv on you."

She had to laugh. "I'm glad you understand that. In my experience guys tend to think it does."

His smile disappeared and she had to wonder why on earth she'd said that.

He pursed his lips. "Milo?"

"Yes, but he's not something I want to talk about. I wanted to forget about that for a while and just enjoy having dinner with you."

"I'd love to. But I don't think it's possible—either to forget or to enjoy dinner if we don't talk about it."

Her heart sank. Maybe he'd brought her back here because he didn't want to dump her in front of everyone. No. That wasn't true, and she knew it. She'd given him the opportunity to walk away, and he'd refused to take it. "I'm sorry."

"It's not your fault."

"I didn't create the situation, no, but you're only in it because of me."

"I'm only in it because I want to be. You gave me the option to leave earlier if you remember."

"I do. And I'm glad you didn't."

He reached across the table and took hold of her hand. "I am, too. You know me. You know I'm not into drama, but I think you're worth it. I don't want to walk away from you, Amber. I want to help you get through this. I want to put it behind us so that we can have a chance."

She reached up and touched his cheek. "Thank you. I want us to have a chance, too. I wish I was a better person. I wish I was stronger. I should have closed the door on him and been straight with my folks long before now."

"That doesn't make you weak." He held her gaze. "But now you have to decide what you want to do."

"I want to stay."

"I know that. I mean you have to decide how you want to handle this." He raised an eyebrow. "Do you want to go along with Jade's lie?"

She shook her head slowly. "I don't think I can."

"Just so you know, I'm willing to do it if you want me to."

Her heart raced in her chest. "You would?"

"Yeah. I'm not comfortable with it. And if it was just Jade, I don't think I would. But the fact that Lenny told me to consider it …" He shook his head. "I've known her all my life. She doesn't stand for any nonsense. I know that. So, if she thinks that this wouldn't be a terrible idea, then I have to believe her." He squeezed her hand. "I'll do whatever you want me to."

She bit her bottom lip. "Lenny's the only reason that I haven't already called them. You're right. She's a wise woman. And I know she cares about me." She frowned. It felt wrong to say it, but she knew it was true. "She cares about me more—and knows me better—than my parents do. If she thinks there's a good reason …"

No. She looked at Austin. She couldn't be … *they* couldn't seriously be considering going along with Jade's lie.

"Maybe you should call her after we eat."

"Yeah. She didn't want to spend her evening with Austin on the phone with her grandmother, but she couldn't see them doing anything else until she figured this out.

~ ~ ~

Austin watched her walk around on the back deck while she talked to Lenny. He rinsed the dishes and set the dishwasher running. He didn't know what to make of all this.

Roscoe came and nosed his leg.

"What's up, buddy?"

Roscoe pawed at him and then went to the patio doors that led out onto the deck.

"No. You can wait in here with me. You need to leave her in peace to talk to Lenny."

Roscoe came back and pawed at his leg again.

"I said, no." Austin smiled. "But I'm glad you like her. She's pretty awesome, huh?"

Roscoe wagged his tail.

"Maybe later we can sit on the sofa and you can sit on the other side of her. Just don't go humping her leg, okay?"

His tail wagged even harder at that, making Austin laugh. Roscoe used to try to hump Nadia any time she sat down here. At first, Austin had thought that he liked her, but over time he figured out that he was smarter than that. She usually left in a huff and expected Austin to go after her to apologize. He used to do it at first, but toward the end of their relationship, he used to let her go, preferring to stay home with Roscoe and only having to listen to her complain over the phone.

Amber came back in and stopped in the doorway.

"What did she say?"

She looked uncomfortable. "She thinks we should do it."

"Why?"

"Same thing she told you. That it'd put a stop to Milo once and for all and that it'd make Mom and Dad understand that I'm really not going back. She's right. I know she is. But I feel like I should do all of that myself—that I already should have ... but I haven't ... so ..."

Austin's heart started to pound. Was she saying that she wanted to go along with it? He raised an eyebrow at her.

She blew out a sigh and came to him. "I don't know! I'm not a liar. I know you aren't. I don't want to put you in that position."

He slid his arms around her waist. "If we're going to consider it, let's consider what it would actually mean."

She looked up at him.

"What would it involve?"

"You'll have to speak to your folks tomorrow one way or another. So, if we do this, that would mean you'd have to lie to them tomorrow. Then … would you talk to them again before they came?"

"Probably not. They'll fly up here on Saturday morning."

"Okay. So, we'd drive down to the airport to get them?"

"Oh. No!" She gave him a worried look. "I … you know I said that they're the kind of people, that money's important to them?"

"Yeah?"

"They fly in a private jet. They don't own it or anything. It's one of those timeshare things where they get to use it so many hours a month. We wouldn't have to pick them up; they'll land right here."

Austin nodded. "Okay. So there wouldn't be an awkward couple of hours in the car with them on the way up here."

She smiled. "No. They'll arrive Saturday morning. They'll want to go straight to the lodge and have some lunch. Then they'll want to come over to the apartment and see how we're keeping it."

He raised an eyebrow at that.

She made a face. "Appearances are important."

He was liking her parents less the more he heard about them. "Okay. Would they want to have dinner with us?"

"Oh, yes That'd be the main interrogation."

He couldn't help but laugh. "Remember I'm trying to figure out if I can stand to do it here. Interrogation doesn't sound too appealing."

She looked serious. "It wouldn't be. It'd be awful. Thanks, Austin, but I just don't think we can—"

His phone started to ring. He didn't want to take it, but she smiled. "Go on. Take it."

He picked it up from the counter to check the display. It wasn't a local number, or anything he recognized. He should probably take it. He looked at Amber and she nodded, then bent down to pet Roscoe. Lucky dog.

"Austin Williams."

"Austin. This is Milo Hall."

"I'm sorry?" He only asked to stall for time. He couldn't believe the guy was calling him.

"Milo Hall," the voice repeated. "Don't tell me you don't know who I am."

He shot a glance at Amber, and as if sensing his unease, she looked up at him.

"I know who you are, Milo."

Her eyes widened, and she came toward him, reaching for the phone. He shook his head.

"So, she told you about me?"

"She did. What can I do for you?"

Amber was watching him wide-eyed.

"It's what I can do for you. I'll let you fuck her one more time, then you can send her on home to me. You might have enjoyed that sweet little pussy for a while, but it belongs to me."

Austin's blood boiled that he could talk about her that way. That any man would talk about a woman that way—a woman he claimed he wanted to marry!

"You hear me? Go find your own woman."

Austin glanced at her. "I have found my own woman. I thought you knew. We're engaged. She's not yours. She's going to marry me."

Amber's hand flew up to cover her mouth and her eyes bulged over the top of it.

"Don't bank on it. Asshole." The line went dead.

"Oh, my God! What did he say? Why did you say that?"

Austin went to her and closed his arms around her. "I'm sorry. I know I just made it worse, but damn, Amber. The guy's a jerk! If you're parents are okay with you being with him, then he has them well and truly fooled." He shook his head. "Fooling them that we're engaged will be easy to do. If they'll fall for that guys spiel, they'll fall for anything."

She looked up at him. "What did he say that made you so mad?"

He shook his head. "It doesn't matter."

She stepped away from him. "It does, Austin. One of the things I value most about you—about the way we are with each other—is that there are no secrets. It feels like we're in it together. I know you think you're protecting me from him, but I don't want to be protected. I want to face it—with you."

He blew out a sigh. "You really want to know?"

"Probably not, if I go by the look on your face. But I need to. Tell me—word for word—what did he say?"

Austin closed his eyes, he'd been about to paraphrase, make it more …

Her eyes bored into him. "I know the way he talks. I'm used to it. You're not going to shock me."

"Okay." He watched her face closely, wondering if she really was used to hearing this kind of thing. "You heard me ask what I could do for him."

She nodded.

"He told me it's what he can do for me. That he'd ..." His fists balled at his sides, but he forced himself to repeat it word for word. "He'd let me fuck you one more time, then I could send you on home to him. That I might have enjoyed that sweet little pussy, but it belongs to him." He couldn't believe he'd said those words to her.

Her face turned bright red.

"I'm sorry. You asked for every word."

She shook her head. "There's no need for you to apologize. If anything, it helps confirm what I've always thought."

"What?"

"That I'm just pussy to him. Well, apart from the in with my parents."

"I'm sorry." Austin didn't know what else he could say.

She gave him a wry smile. "I guess you were right about me being sweet, huh?" She was trying to make a joke out of it. Trying to lighten the moment.

He didn't feel very light. But he went along with her. "You are."

She let out a little laugh. "And at least he thought you'd want one more go, before you sent me back."

He raised an eyebrow at her. "I'm still waiting for the first go."

Her cheeks colored up again, but she smiled. "What do you think. Is it official now? There's no way I'm going back."

Austin pursed his lips. "I was only joking around with you. Trying to make you smile again."

"I know. But …" She let the words trail off and looked up into his eyes.

"It'd be hard to say no, but I think we have more pressing matters to deal with first."

"We do."

"I think I committed us to going along with Jade's lie, didn't I?"

She nodded. "I think you did."

"And you're not mad at me?"

"How could I be mad? You only did it to defend me."

"I'm sorry. I couldn't listen to him talk about you like that. And when he said you belonged to him."

"I don't."

"I know."

Roscoe chose that moment to stick his nose up her skirt again. At least it made her laugh.

"Shall we have another glass of wine and take it outside?" she asked.

He nodded slowly. "If I have another one I won't be able to take you home."

She held his gaze for a long moment and then smiled. "That's okay."

~ ~ ~

Amber's heart started to race. Did he understand what she meant? She wasn't telling him that she wouldn't mind having to take a cab. She was saying that she wanted to stay with him.

He poured their wine and she followed him back out onto the deck. She sat on the sofa, but he didn't come and sit beside her. He took one of the chairs instead.

She took a sip of her wine and stared out at the beautiful view. The lake shimmered in the late evening sun.

He gave her rueful smile. "Are you sure you're not mad at me? I know you don't want to have to lie to your parents."

"I'm not mad. I'm grateful to you. Thank you."

"Of course."

"Are you mad at me?"

"No. Why would I be?"

"Like you said earlier, you don't like drama. I don't either, but I seem to have landed us in the middle of it with all this."

He smiled. "You're the only one who hasn't caused any of it. Jade started it. Milo made it worse by calling me, and then I exacerbated the situation."

She blew out a sigh. "But it's all because of me. And now you're sitting over there."

He smiled through pursed lips. "I'm sitting over here because of what you said before we came out." Her tummy flipped over at the way he looked at her. "You don't mind me having another drink—which means I can't drive you home."

She nodded. "And just so we're clear, I don't plan on calling a cab."

He shifted in his seat. "I didn't for a moment think that you did." He chuckled. "And that's why I'm over here. If I sat next to you right now, I'd be as bad as Roscoe."

She laughed out loud at that, glad to relieve the tension. "You'd stick your head up my skirt?"

He laughed with her. "Not that exactly, though it's tempting."

Shivers chased each other down her spine at the thought of it.

Austin looked more serious now, though. "I ... I can't believe I'm going to say this, but I think it'd be better if we wait."

Her heart sank. "Why?"

"Because when we go there, I want it to be about us."

She frowned. "What else would it be about?"

He made a face. "I just got off the phone with your ex, remember? He gave me his blessing to sleep with you."

"Oh." She nodded sadly. "I hate that he can throw a shadow over us—over what happens between us."

Austin got up and came to sit beside her. "I do too. I don't want him to. That's why I'd rather wait. I'd rather we got there in our time."

He ran his fingers down her bare arm, making her wonder how she was supposed to wait.

She gave him a sad smile. "Are you saying I should call a cab?"

He held her gaze for a moment and then smiled. "You can if you want, but I'd rather you didn't."

"I don't understand."

He dropped a kiss on her lips. "You can stay. I'd like you to. Just because we're not going to sleep together, doesn't mean that we can't hang out."

"For the night?"

He nodded. "Yeah."

She smiled back at him. "Okay."

He set his glass down on the table and leaned back against the sofa. She set hers down and leaned against him. His arm curled around her, and she looked up into his eyes. "Do you think we need to figure out how we're going to play this whole thing?"

"I do, but not now. Not tonight. I want tonight, or at least, what's left of it, to be about you and me."

She slid her arms up around his neck. She liked the sound of that. He lowered his head until his lips brushed over hers. He made her feel so many things. He made her feel safe in a way that she wasn't used to.

As his tongue slid inside her mouth and he kissed her more deeply, he made her feel sexy. He crushed her against his hard chest and his hand roved over her, grazing her breast, squeezing her ass—he made her feel aroused. But knowing that they weren't going to go there—weren't going to do that, tonight made her feel relaxed. She hadn't made out with a guy and known that he wasn't going to try and take it further since high school. Of course, she wanted him; she was aching for him, but one part of her was glad that there was no pressure. She lay back on the sofa, and he came with her, pressing himself between her legs, making her moan into his mouth. If this was his way of making sure that she'd want him desperately by the time he finally made love to her, he was doing a good job of it.

# Chapter Thirteen

When Austin opened his eyes, he stared up at the ceiling. He hadn't thought he'd be able to sleep at all. Not here, alone in his bed, with Amber just down the hall in the guest bedroom. He blew out a sigh and rolled onto his side.

Was he some kind of idiot? He was starting to think he must be. He'd had more than one opportunity to sleep with her— and he kept putting it off. She would have willingly come to bed with him last night. She wanted to. He knew it. But it wouldn't have been right. Even while they were making out on the sofa, he'd kept hearing Milo's voice echo in his head. *I'll let you fuck her.* It made him shudder. That asshole should have nothing to do with anything that happened between Amber and him. But if they'd had sex last night, the thought of him would be hanging over their heads. It wasn't right.

That wasn't how he wanted to begin things with Amber, and he was seeing this as the beginning of something—hopefully, something special. Granted, lying to her parents wasn't a great start. Pretending to be her fiancé … He shook his head. What had he gotten himself into?

The bedroom door opened a crack and his breath caught in his chest. If she came in here now ... His cock woke up in a hurry and stood to attention at the possibility.

He let his breath out in short laugh when Roscoe came in.

"Come here, boy." He patted the bed.

Roscoe jumped up and came and licked his face.

"Morning buddy. Where've you been?" He gave him a stern look. "Don't tell me you went in there with her?"

Roscoe panted at him, looking pleased with himself.

"Don't look at me like that you old perv. I hope you didn't try to hump her." Even as he said it, Austin realized he wouldn't blame him if he had.

He sat up at the sound of movement in the hallway. "Are you up, Amber?"

"Yeah. Sorry. I didn't mean to disturb you."

"It's okay. I'm awake. I'll be right out." He rolled out of bed and pulled on a pair of sweatpants and hurried into the bathroom.

She was making coffee when he got to the kitchen.

"Here, let me do that." He reached around and took the pot from her.

Her eyes widened as she turned to look up at him.

"Sorry. I didn't mean to startle you."

She dropped her gaze, but her lips quirked up into a little smile. "I just didn't expect to come face to face with your bare chest before I'm even properly awake."

"Oh." He hadn't even thought to put a shirt on. "Sorry."

She looked up into his eyes. "I'm not."

She stepped closer, and he slid his arms around her, cursing himself again for not having taken her to bed last night. She felt so warm and soft—making him feel hot and hard. He closed his eyes and rested his chin on top of her head. Damn, he wanted her.

She stepped away from him with a rueful smile. "Sorry."

He chuckled. "Not as sorry as I am."

She raised an eyebrow, and he nodded.

"I'm not going to say what I'm thinking. I'm sure you can guess. What I will say is that I hope you don't have other plans tonight?"

"I don't." Her cheeks were touched with pink, but there was no hesitation in her voice.

"Good." He got on with making the coffee. He turned to smile at her as a thought struck him. "I was about to say I'll go and put a shirt on, but now that I think about it ... you should probably get used to seeing your fiancé's naked chest."

She chuckled and let her gaze travel over him, making him ache for her. "I'd be happy to."

"Good." He wanted to close his arms around her again. Wanted to undress her and finally get to see her naked chest, but this wasn't the time. He needed to find out what she wanted to do with the day—he was hoping that she wanted to spend it with him, but he didn't know that yet.

~ ~ ~

They drank their coffee sitting out on the deck. "It's so beautiful here." Amber couldn't get enough of the view. She shot a sideways glance at Austin. The mountains and the lake were beautiful, but they paled in comparison to him.

He didn't notice the way she was looking at him—and that was probably a good thing, she was all but licking her lips at the sight of his lean, muscled chest, and those arms ... She took a big gulp of her coffee and burned her mouth. It served her right!

"I'm glad you like it. I love this place. What do you want to do today?"

"I need to go home and get changed." She was hoping that they might do something together, but she didn't know what his plans were.

"Do you want to go soon?"

She nodded sadly. He probably had work to do. He'd need to take her home.

"Hey." He touched her arm. "I don't mean I want to take you home and leave you there. I'd like to take you to breakfast—if you want to go? I …" He looked wary. "I wondered if you want to spend the day with me?"

"I'd love to!" She laughed. "Sorry. I was hoping, but then I thought maybe you had to go to work."

"No. Well, I do have to show a place this afternoon, but that'll only take me an hour. I could drop you home while I go and then pick you up afterward, if you like?"

"That'd be great. I have a few things I need to take care of, too."

"Are you going to call your parents?"

"Yeah." She blew out a sigh. "Are you sure—?"

"I'm sure. I was thinking about it last night." He smiled through pursed lips. "While I was lying there awake."

She had to laugh at that, she'd spent most of the night tossing and turning and wishing that she had the nerve to go into his bedroom. "You, too, huh?"

He smiled at her. "You were the same?"

She nodded. It felt good to admit it to him. "I barely slept a wink."

He laughed.

She sucked in a deep breath, but she needed to say it. "And I don't plan on sleeping much tonight either."

He chuckled and slid his arm around her shoulders. "That's good because I don't plan on letting you."

A rush of heat swept through her. So, tonight would be the night. She couldn't wait!

When they got to the apartment, he leaned across the console and dropped a kiss on her lips. "How long do you need?"

She gave him a puzzled look. "You don't want to come in?"

"I didn't want to invite myself."

She laughed. "If you're going to be my fiancé, then you should probably know your way around my apartment. Oh, but I guess you already do, don't you?"

He nodded.

"Have you managed it for long? Who owns it?"

He smiled.

"Oh! You do?"

He nodded. "I rented it myself while I was remodeling the house, and when I left, the owners wanted to sell. It's a good place, and I know its history."

She smiled. "Well, I guess we won't need to worry about you knowing your way around when my folks come then."

"No." He looked uncomfortable now. "I suppose we should spend some time figuring out what else I should know before I meet them."

Amber's smile faded. "Yeah. We should." She shook her head. "You have to promise me that you'll tell me if you want to change your mind."

He squeezed her hand. "I won't."

"Okay. Come on up then. I need a quick shower, but I won't take long. And then you have to let me buy you breakfast."

He raised an eyebrow.

"You've taken care of everything so far. I don't want you to feel that you always have to."

"Okay. Thanks."

Austin looked around the apartment. He was surprised how neat and tidy everything was. He'd kind of expected two sisters to be messy. He wouldn't normally go inside one of his properties without giving the tenants at least forty-eight hours' notice. He was only required to give twenty-four, but he didn't like to do that. As far as he was concerned, he was going into someone's home—and in your home you should be able to relax and have a mess if that was how you lived.

He started when the front door opened. Jade came in and raised an eyebrow at him.

"Morning. You're here early. Or …"

He smiled. "I'm here early."

"Cool. Did you guys figure things out last night?"

He nodded slowly. He wasn't sure it was his place to tell her about his conversation with Milo.

He was relieved when Amber came out of her room. Her hair was still wet, but she was dressed.

Jade looked at her. "What did you guys decide?"

Amber looked at Austin. He loved that she wanted to check with him before she spoke.

Jade laughed. "Whatever it is, you're in it together, right?"

Amber nodded. "Yeah. Milo kind of made sure of that."

"What do you mean?"

"He called Austin last night."

Jade turned to him. "What did he say?"

Austin was hardly going to repeat it. He looked at Amber. "Basically, he told me that he hoped I'd had fun with Amber, but that I need to send her back to him now—because she's his."

"Jesus! He is unbelievable. What did you say?"

He gave Jade a wry smile. "I'm afraid he pushed my buttons. I told him that she wouldn't be coming back. That she doesn't belong to him ... And that we're engaged."

Jade laughed. "Why do I get the impression that the conversation wasn't as civil as you're making it sound?"

"It wasn't."

"No," said Amber. "Austin's putting it nicely." She shot him a grateful smile, and he was glad he'd given Jade the G-rated version.

Jade made a face. "I hate to think what he really said."

Austin nodded, but didn't comment.

Jade looked at Amber. "Does this mean that you're going to go along with it?"

Amber nodded.

Jade turned to Austin. "And you're okay with it?"

"Yeah."

"Awesome! So, what happens now? Are you guys going to spend the week at your place?"

Amber frowned. "Why?"

Jade shot Austin a smile before going to Amber. "Because, sweet little sister, if you're going to be able to convince Mom and Dad that you two are engaged, you should probably be more relaxed around each other than you are. And if they're going to go over to Austin's place, you want to look like you're used to being there." She glanced back at Austin with a smirk on her face. "Right?"

Austin didn't know what to think. She had a point, but … he had to smile. Why did there have to be a but? He'd love it if Amber wanted to spend the week with him. He met her gaze. She looked uncertain, but he got the feeling that that was more about what he might think.

He made his decision and nodded. If they were going to go through with it, they might as well make the most of it. "She has a point, you know. We already said that we should spend some time getting to know each other better."

Jade looked as though she was about to laugh. And Austin could guess why—she knew what kind of getting to know each other he was thinking about.

To his relief, Amber smiled. "Well, if you don't mind …" Her smile faded. "I hadn't thought about it, but they are going to want to see your place—and they are going to judge you by it."

Jade glanced at him.

He could hardly tell her that they'd no doubt be impressed.

Amber had no such reservations. She smiled at her sister. "That's the first thing that they'll love about him."

"Yeah?" She looked at Austin. "Sorry, but Milo lives in a McMansion in one of the best neighborhoods. That's hard to beat in our parents' eyes."

Amber came to him with an apologetic look on her face. "God. I'm sorry. I feel terrible."

He slid his arm around her. He didn't want her to feel that way. He knew she wasn't attracted to him because of what he had. It wasn't her fault that he'd go up in her parents' estimation because he owned a nice house. "It's okay, sweetie.

It doesn't bother me." He smiled down at her. "In fact, I'm pleased that I can now finally feel justified in buying a house that's way too much for just one guy."

Jade laughed. "Will one of you fill me in?"

"Milo's place is about half the size of Austin's. And Austin's up in the hills with an amazing view." Amber glanced at him. "And a huge pool that I haven't got to swim in yet."

He laughed. "Bring your swimsuit."

Jade waggled her eyebrows. "Or don't."

Austin liked that idea, but he was hardly going to say so in front of Jade. He was going along with this whole fiancé thing against his better judgment. But he needed Jade to understand that this was about more than that for him.

~ ~ ~

Austin took hold of her hand as they walked out across the deck of the restaurant. It made her smile. Most of their friends would be here; breakfast at the Boathouse was just something everyone did on the weekends. She was glad she didn't have to wonder if he minded them seeing him with her—knowing that they were together.

He smiled at her. "Is this okay?"

"It's wonderful. Are you ready to face everyone?"

"I'm ready for them to know that we're together—though, to be fair, they've kind of been waiting for it."

She nodded, glad that he knew it and didn't mind acknowledging it.

He pursed his lips. "We should have cleared it up before we got here, but what do you want to say?"

"About …? Oh." She sighed. "I don't know. We don't need to say anything yet, do we? Or do you want to?"

"I'd rather not ... not yet. It's no one else's business. But at the same time, I don't want to hide it. I think I'd rather we have a better idea of what we're doing ourselves before we face a barrage of questions."

"Yeah." She knew he was right. They'd all want to know more.

He squeezed her hand. "One step at a time. They're all going to be happy to see us here together. Let's just roll with that for now."

"Austin Williams!" It was Logan who greeted them first with a big grin on his face. Amber liked him. He was fun, but he could be a bit over-the-top.

Austin tightened his grip on her hand. "Logan Perkins. What can I do for you?"

Logan winked at Amber. "You can tell us all how you finally managed to get your act together and show up here for breakfast with the lovely Amber."

She felt heat in her cheeks. It was only natural that they'd assume that showing up for breakfast together meant that they'd spent the night together. And she had spent the night at his place. She just wished that Logan was right, and she'd spent it in his bed.

Austin didn't get the chance to answer. Luke punched Logan's arm. "Leave him alone."

Logan's fiancée, Roxy, rolled her eyes at Amber. "Sorry. I can't take him anywhere."

"Come sit down, guys." Abbie, who was sitting at the other end of the long picnic table smiled and patted the space beside her. "I can rescue you from nosey Perkins," she shot Logan an evil look, "and if you don't mind, I want to pick your brains, Austin."

Amber sat next to Abbie, and Austin slid in next to her fiancé, Ivan, opposite them.

Ivan grinned. "Don't worry, I'm not going to embarrass you. I just want to say I'm happy to see you here together."

"Thanks." Austin smiled at Amber. "Not as happy as I am."

"Aww." Abbie nudged Amber's arm. "I grew up with these guys, and I have to tell you, you've landed yourself the best one in Summer Lake."

"Excuse me?" Ivan gave her a mock hurt look, but she just laughed.

"You know what I mean. The best of the ones who grew up here. Obviously, I have the best guy in town."

Ivan laughed. "Okay, I'll let you off."

The server came out and poured coffee and took their orders. Once he'd gone, Abbie turned to Austin.

"I know I shouldn't pester you about work on the weekend, but I wanted to ask you about rental properties."

"What about them?" Austin smiled at Ivan. "I know you two aren't thinking of renting. Your place is one of the nicest on the water."

Ivan smiled back at him. "Nope. We're set for life, right, Abbs?"

Amber got a warm and fuzzy feeling as she watched Abbie rest her head against Ivan's shoulder. She had to wonder what it would be like to be so totally in love and so confident in your man.

"You got that right." Abbie reached up and kissed Ivan's cheek. "You've been sentenced to a lifetime with me." She turned back to Austin. "It's about my mom's place. I've been nagging her to rent it out. I don't mind keeping an eye on it for her, but she could be making some money on it while she's not here."

Austin nodded. "Would she rent it out long-term?"

"No, that's the trouble. I told her we'd put everything in storage for her, and she could put it up as an annual unfurnished rental, but she doesn't want to do that. She still wants to come back and be able to stay there sometimes."

"Hmm. So, she'd want to do vacation rentals?"

"That's what she said, but I wanted to ask what you think. It's not really a vacation type of house, is it?"

"No, but I might be able to help her out, at least with something short-term to get her started. I talked to a guy the other day—I know him, Zack does, too, so it wouldn't just be some random stranger. He's thinking about moving up here, and he wants to rent somewhere that'd give him an idea of what it'd be like to live here—not just visit on vacation."

Abbie nodded. "That sounds perfect. If he wants to see what it's like to live in a regular house on a regular street, then my mom's place would be ideal for him. How long does he want to stay?"

"He said he'd like to try a month at first."

"Awesome. Do you know when?"

"Not for another few weeks. He said next month originally, but he had some other plans fall through, and he might want to come sooner. I'm waiting to hear back from him. There's not much available that'd work at the moment; all the vacation rentals are booked out."

"Well, I'm pretty sure Mom would be okay with it—depending on when it is."

"Do you vet people who are only staying short term?" asked Ivan.

Amber loved that he was looking out for Abbie's mom. She didn't know him that well, but he seemed like a good guy, and she knew he'd helped Abbie and her mom through a rough time.

Austin was smiling. "I don't, no. It just wouldn't be practical for short-term rentals. But I can assure you that you have nothing to worry about with Manny. Like I said, I know him, Zack knows him, Zack's dad knows him. And if we're not enough to vouch for his character then perhaps the fact that he's the special agent in charge of the FBI field office in Sacramento might be enough to convince you."

Ivan laughed. "Okay. I'm good with that."

Abbie wasn't smiling anymore. "Do you think he'd want to stay at my mom's place?"

Ivan put his arm around her shoulders. "He'd be lucky to. It's a great little house."

"It is," said Austin. "I know what you're thinking, but Manny's not looking for anything fancy. He's getting ready to take early retirement, and he just wants to live a peaceful life in a place where he already knows a few people."

"Okay. Well, I'll talk to Mom and see what she thinks and then … what? Should I take some pictures or …"

"How about I come over one day in the week? I can take a look at the place, and we can get some photos."

"Great." Abbie smiled at Amber. "Sorry, I didn't mean to drag him into work conversation."

Amber smiled. "It's not a problem. I like hearing about it."

"What about you?" asked Ivan. "What are you going to do for work?"

"I'm still at the post office."

"I know but I thought now that Lenny's back on her feet ... Does she still need you and Jade?"

"She needs someone. She wants to go part-time. She's asked if I want to stay on."

She could feel Austin watching her and realized that she hadn't told him that yet. She also remembered that she shouldn't be getting too relaxed. There was a lot she'd have to get him up to speed on about herself and her life if they were going to be able to fool her parents next weekend. And there was the minor detail that she had to call them and face the music about having supposedly gotten engaged without even telling them she'd met someone.

# Chapter Fourteen

It was almost noon by the time they left the Boathouse. Most of the gang had the morning free, and they'd all ended up sitting out on the deck hanging out and catching up for hours. Austin loved it. And he knew Amber had too. His life had always been here. He loved Summer Lake, and he loved that he helped other people to become part of it—helped them find homes to live in. He hoped that she was going to grow to see this place as home. He'd helped her find the apartment she lived in now, and … no, he wasn't even going to think about maybe helping her find her next home.

She looked up at him as they walked back across the square to his truck. "What time do you have to go to work?"

He'd forgotten that he had a showing to do. He laughed. "It's a good thing you reminded me. I have to show a house at one-thirty."

"Okay. What do you want to do then? There's no point going all the way back out to your house and then coming back again."

She seemed edgy.

He put his arm around her shoulders. "What do you want to do? Are you okay?"

"Yeah." She blew out a sigh. "I'll be better after I call my parents, though."

"Damn! I'm sorry, sweetie. I was having such a good time this morning, I forgot. You should have said. We could have left."

"No! I was enjoying myself, too. I completely forgot about it—which just shows you how much I was enjoying myself. But now that we have to decide what to do next, I can't do anything until I've talked to them. I'm dreading it, but I don't want to put it off any longer. If I don't call them soon, they're bound to call me."

He nodded. "Do you want me to leave you to it? Would you rather I'm with you?" He didn't know how she'd want to play it, but he wanted to support her in whatever way he could.

She smiled. "I think I'd rather do it by myself. Maybe you could drop me off at the apartment? I'll call them and catch up on a few things at home while you go to work."

"Okay." He should probably check in at the office anyway. "I'll call you when I get done and see if you're ready to head back to my place?"

"Oh, I'm sure I'll be more than ready."

He smiled. "Do you want to bring your PJ's and your toothbrush this time?" As soon as the words were out, he wished he'd said it differently. He sounded like a kid inviting his friend for a sleepover.

She seemed to like it though. Her eyes shone as she nodded. "I would."

"And don't forget your swimsuit."

She waggled her eyebrows, and he knew that she was remembering what Jade had said—or not!

They reached the SUV, and he held the door open for her. Another few hours—that was all he'd have to wait now. He'd get through his appointment. She'd face her parents, and they'd be free to spend the afternoon—the rest of the weekend—together. He shifted in his seat as he pulled out onto Main Street. They could hang out, spend some time in the pool, and hopefully, some time in bed.

~ ~ ~

Amber let herself into the apartment and went to the window to wave at Austin as he drove away. Her chest flooded with warmth when he blew her a kiss, and she blew him one back. He was wonderful!

She spun around at the sound of Jade laughing. "You're so loved up you didn't even notice me!"

"I didn't, sorry. I'm not going to deny it."

"Good. He's awesome."

"He is."

"So, what are you doing back here?"

She blew out a sigh. "I've come to face the music. I'm going to call Mom and Dad."

"Shit! You haven't talked to them yet?"

"Nope."

"Ugh. You'd better do it then. Get it over with."

"I know. What exactly did you tell them?"

"I didn't really say much to them. I told Milo that you'd met a great guy who'd swept you off your feet. That he's really good to you and you're head over heels in love with him. And he's asked you to marry him."

"And what did Dad say?"

"He wanted to know why you hadn't said anything to them. I told them that it'd all happened so fast, and I told them that you know they like Milo and you didn't want to disappoint them."

Amber made a face.

"I thought I might as well try and get some truth in there."

"What did he have to say about that?"

Jade cringed. "He said you'd disappointed him by not telling them … and that he was disappointed that this Austin guy hadn't asked for his permission first … like Milo did."

"Oh, crap! I didn't even think about that."

"Neither did I, but it's not a big deal, is it? It's just some old-fashioned tradition."

"Not to Dad." Amber didn't like to say it to her sister, but she suspected that Austin was the kind of guy who would honor that old-fashioned tradition—if he got the chance. Well, if he ever asked a girl to marry him. It wasn't as though he'd actually asked her.

"What's up?"

She shook her head. "Nothing. I was just being stupid. I know we only just started seeing each other, and who knows where it might go. But I just realized that … nothing."

Jade smiled. "Are you wishing that he had asked Dad's permission, for real?"

She shrugged. "It's stupid. I know. I just got carried away for a minute."

"It's not stupid. I think it's quite likely. Which just makes me feel even worse for running my mouth in the first place."

"Don't feel bad. You meant well. I know that."

"I did. But come on. Make the call. Once it's done, you can relax a bit until this time next week when they come. If you ask me, I think you should spend the week with Austin at his place. Get to know each other so you'll be more convincing."

Amber smiled through pursed lips. "I wouldn't mind."

Jade laughed. "I knew it! You should do it. You can spend the whole week role-playing what engaged couples do."

Amber had to laugh. "I'd love to. But it wouldn't be right. It wouldn't be fair to Austin."

"Ha! Wouldn't be fair? The poor guy must have the bluest balls on the planet right now. You didn't sleep with him last night, did you? You haven't slept with him yet?"

"No."

"And it was obvious, that he wanted to do you the first time you met! How would it not be fair to put yourself in his bed every night for the next week? I think it's only fair. He's going along with this for you—the least you could do is show a little gratitude."

Amber chuckled. "I'm grateful, all right. And I plan to show him how much tonight."

"You do? That's awesome. And once you have, there's no reason you shouldn't keep doing it."

"I'd love to. But you keep distracting me. What I need to do is call Mom and Dad."

"Yeah. Sorry. Do you want me to go out?"

She shook her head. "No. You can stay."

~ ~ ~

Austin let himself into the office and smiled at Crystal. "How's it going?"

"Better, now that you're here. I was starting to think you must have forgotten about your one-thirty."

He checked his watch. "It's not even one yet."

She laughed. "I know. But you're usually here a couple of hours before a showing unless you're out on another one."

"Yeah. I was busy this morning."

She glanced up at him. "I heard."

"Let me guess, the whole town noticed that we all stayed at the Boathouse all morning?"

She shook her head. "Your brother told me that he wasn't allowed to go home last night."

Austin pursed his lips. "He's been in here then?"

She nodded.

He didn't have many reservations about bringing Dallas in to work with him, but he did have a few. One of them was about the way Dallas was with women. He had a way with them, no doubt about it. But he wasn't into anything serious, or long term. He charmed them, slept with them, and then moved on. Crystal had taken a shine to him the last time he'd been home to visit. That was a complication Austin didn't need.

Crystal ran the office for him—and she ran it like a well-oiled machine. He didn't need Dallas having his way with her and upsetting things around here.

"Problem?" she asked.

"I hope not."

"He told me that he's going to be working with you."

"How would you feel about that?"

She smiled. "He's fun."

He gave her a stern look. "I know it's not my place to say anything. But if you had fun with him, it wouldn't last for long."

She smiled through pursed lips. "Who says I'd want it to?"

"Oh." He didn't know what to say to that.

She laughed. "Sorry, Austin I couldn't help it. You're such a stand-up guy, and you think everyone else lives up to your high moral standards. I don't like to disappoint you, but I'm not one of those women who's looking to hook a guy and get married. I just want to have some fun—and your brother seems like he'd be a lot of fun."

Austin held his hands up. "Okay. If you don't think it'd be a problem ..."

"It wouldn't. And I hope you're not disappointed in me."

"Why would I be?"

She shrugged. "You're just like the perfect guy. You do everything right, and here I am admitting that I'm not above having a bit of fun for the sake of fun."

He had to smile. "Whatever makes you think I'm perfect, you couldn't be further from the truth. I don't do everything right. In fact, right now. I'm in the middle of doing something very wrong." He chuckled. "And just so we're clear. I like fun as much as the next guy."

She smiled. "Sure, you do, but to you it's not fun unless it means something more. I probably shouldn't say anything, and I'll shut my mouth after this, but I heard about you and Amber. I think that's awesome. She's a sweetheart. You deserve someone like her. I'm so glad you finally got rid of Nadia."

He had to smile. He'd broken up with Nadia months ago, and Crystal had never said a word. They had a great working relationship. She was the same age as him, and an attractive woman, according to some of his friends, but he didn't see her as a woman. She was an employee, technically. A colleague in his mind. And their relationship had always been professional. In fact, this conversation was as personal as it had ever gotten.

"Did I say too much?"

"No. I'm glad you spoke up."

She smiled. "Me, too. I'm not going to expect you to start sitting and chatting with me. But if Dallas is going to come and join the team, things will change a bit around here, and I'm glad to know that we're straight with each other before they do."

"Yeah. Me, too."

She handed him a file. "This is everything we have on the place you're showing the Kellys this afternoon, and the sellers have just dropped the price on the one you showed them out on East Shore last weekend. You said that they liked it, but it was over their budget. They might want to revisit it now."

"Thanks, Crystal." He took the file. "I'll give them a call and see what they think. We could stop into the one on East Shore first if they want to take another look."

"Okay. I'll be out here if you need me."

Austin went into his office and closed the door. He opened the file and then blew out a sigh. Things were getting away from him. He was supposed to have gotten in touch with Kenzie and Chase this week, and it had totally slipped his mind. It'd taken Crystal to let him know about the price drop on the house the Kellys were interested in. And he hadn't followed up with Dallas about work—or about getting him set up with his own place.

He'd been distracted. Every spare moment he had, he'd been thinking about Amber. If she was going to stay with him for the next week like Jade had suggested, he'd no doubt be even more distracted. He should get ahead of things while he could.

By the time he was ready to go and meet the Kellys, he had appointments lined up with Kenzie and Chase and with Abbie at her mom's place. He'd left Dallas a message to call him—they needed to talk about getting him set up with own place as soon as possible.

"Will you be back?" asked Crystal.

"No. I've caught up on what I needed to and the Kellys are the only appointment I have this afternoon." He smiled. "Why don't you close up and take the afternoon off?"

She raised an eyebrow at him.

He shrugged. "Of course, you can stay if you want to …"

She laughed. "Err, no. I'll get out of here if you really don't mind. I'll forward the phone to my cell, though—just in case."

"Great. Thanks. I'll see you Monday then. You have a good weekend."

"Thanks, Austin. You, too."

He couldn't help smiling to himself as he drove away. He planned to have a very good weekend indeed just as soon as he picked Amber up. His smile faded when he remembered what she was doing right now. She'd be talking to her parents. He'd deal with that whole situation next weekend when they came to visit. It didn't have to spoil this weekend.

Amber dialed her Dad's number and made a face at Jade while it rang.

"Amber."

"Hi, Dad."

"I'm surprised at you. I might have expected something like this from your sister, but not you."

"I'm sorry. It just all happened so quickly."

"It must have. Don't you think you're being hasty, agreeing to marry someone you barely know?"

"I do know him, Dad." She smiled at Jade. "He's wonderful." At least, she didn't need to lie about that.

"I'll be the judge of that. And besides, you know you have a wonderful man here who wants to marry you."

Her heart sank. She wished her dad could see that Milo wasn't nearly as wonderful as he believed. She had to wonder what he'd think if she told him exactly what Milo had said to Austin about her. "Milo's not the one for me, Dad. I tried to tell you that before. I know you think he's good for the business. I'm not even sure I agree about that, but that's your call to make. He's not good for me. You might not agree, but that's my call to make."

Jade gave her the thumbs up at that.

Her dad sighed. "I'd never try to force you to stay with him if he doesn't make you happy. I thought he did."

Amber gave Jade a surprised look, and Jade pointed at the phone, she wanted her to put him on speaker.

Amber hit the button and set the phone down. "I'm sorry. That's my fault. I know you like him, and I didn't want to disappoint you or make things difficult so I didn't say much, but he didn't make me happy. In fact, he made me miserable."

"I'm sorry, sweetheart."

Amber's eyes filled with tears. "It's not your fault, Dad. I messed things up by trying to do what I thought you wanted. I wanted to make you happy."

He sighed. "I know. You've always done that. I wish you wouldn't. What would make your mom and me happy is you doing whatever you need to make yourself happy. That's all we've ever wanted for you."

Amber sniffed. She felt stupid. "I'm sorry."

"Don't be sorry; be different. Do what you need to do. Take a leaf out of your sister's book."

Jade nodded at her happily.

"If you're done with Milo, then that's fine by me."

She blew out a big sigh of relief. "Thanks, Dad. Will it make things awkward for you at work, though?"

"No. I ..." He was quiet for a long moment.

"What?"

"To be honest with you, I've been questioning just how good he is since you left."

Jade nodded vigorously and mouthed, *tell him!*

Amber pursed her lips. She didn't want to throw Milo under the bus, but then it struck her. If she didn't, she was pretty much throwing her dad under. She took a deep breath. "I'm not saying this to be vindictive, but now that you know that I don't want to come back, you should probably keep an eye on him—and on how things get done. I used to do a lot more than he let on."

Her dad sighed. "I'd started to figure that out for myself. There've been a few issues since you've been gone."

Amber didn't know what to say.

"But you know what? That really isn't your problem. You're done with him. That's all we need to know. We never wanted you to feel tied to the business, you know."

"You didn't?"

He let out a short laugh. "No! You silly girl. We wanted it to provide for you if you wanted, and you never led us to believe that you didn't want it."

"I'm sorry. I didn't want to let you down."

"You couldn't, not if you're doing what makes you happy. And speaking of which, Mom tells me that you want to stay on at the post office. Would that make you happy?"

"Yes. I'm enjoying myself there."

"And this Austin—he makes you happy?"

"He does, Dad. I think you'll like him."

"We'll see about that next weekend."

She sucked in a deep breath. "You will."

"What do I need to know about him?"

Amber thought about it for a moment. She wanted to say that he was kind and generous, that he was a good man and he was good to her, but she didn't think that was the kind of thing her dad wanted to know.

Instead, she went with, "He's a realtor. He has his own brokerage. He also does property management and he owns several rental properties. In fact, he owns the apartment Jade and I are living in."

"He's your landlord?"

Amber made a face at her sister. That had probably sounded wrong. "Yes. He was one of the first people we met when we came up here."

"I don't like the sound of that."

She rolled her eyes. She'd gone for what she thought might impress him and still messed it up. "You should ask Lenny. She'll vouch for him. She's known him all his life."

Her dad let out a short laugh. "Don't worry. She's told me all about how wonderful she thinks he is, but remember that your grandmother and I don't always see eye to eye."

It was true. Amber had forgotten that.

"Well, if you won't take my word, or hers, then I guess you'll just have to judge for yourself next weekend."

"I intend to. And your mother."

"How is she? Is she there?" Amber had expected that they'd both want to talk to her.

"No. She's out."

"Is she mad at me?"

Her dad sighed. "I wish you'd give us some credit, love. She's worried about you, not mad at you."

Amber felt bad. "Well do me a favor and tell her she has nothing to worry about. She'll see next weekend. You both will."

"We will. And I have to tell you, Amber, we'll let you know if we think you're making a mistake."

She couldn't help letting out a little laugh at that. "Oh, I know you will. But I think you're going to be pleasantly surprised."

"I'm open to that, but I'm not holding my breath. Anyway, I need to get going. We'll see you next Saturday."

"Okay. Let me know what time you're landing? I'll come and pick you up at the airport."

"That's okay. I've booked a car. We'll come and see you."

"I guess we'd better tidy the apartment then." She wanted to joke with him and leave things on a lighter note.

He didn't go along with it. "I'm not stupid, Amber. I want to see where you're really living. We'll expect to come over to this Austin's place."

Jade smiled and nodded at that, and Amber couldn't help but smile back, knowing that Austin's house would impress them. Her smile faded as she wished that they'd be impressed by more important things.

She wondered if she should argue and tell him that she wasn't already living there, but she knew there'd be no point. "Okay."

"Okay then. I'll call you and let you know what time we'll be landing."

"Okay. See you next week. I love you, Dad."

He sighed. "I love you, too, Amber. We don't seem to do that in a way you understand, but we do love you."

"I know."

"Bye then."

When she hung up, she made a face at Jade.

"What? That went way better than I thought it would."

"I suppose."

"What's up then?"

Amber shrugged. "I don't know. I wish I wasn't lying to them. I wish I'd had that conversation with him about Milo months ago. I should have done it as soon as I left."

"Yeah, you should. But better late than never, right?"

"I suppose."

"Come on, cheer up. It's over with now."

She blew out a sigh. "It isn't! It's just beginning. This time next week, they'll be here. And I'll have to lie to their faces, and so will Austin."

"Yeah, but only for a couple of days and then they'll be gone, and you'll be free."

It was true. Even though Amber felt bad about lying to her parents, she did feel relieved that she'd finally been clear with them that she and Milo were over and that she wouldn't be getting back with him.

"What time's Austin coming back for you?"

"He said probably about two-thirty after he's done showing a house."

"Good. Then why don't we pack you a bag for the week—and put all your sexiest undies in it?"

She had to laugh. "I'm not going to pack for the week. I'm staying there tonight, then we'll see."

"Are you telling me that you wouldn't want to spend the week with him—even if it wouldn't be helpful to know your way around his place before the folks come?"

"No. I was going to say I'm not a liar, but apparently, these days I am. I won't lie about that though. Of course, I'd love to spend the week with him, but he hasn't asked me to. It's better to see how tonight goes and then take it from there."

Jade laughed. "Okay, then we'll just pack your sexiest undies for tonight—and maybe while you're gone, I'll pack you another bag for the rest of the week so it's ready for when he asks. You know he's going to ask."

Amber couldn't help but smile. She didn't know that he would—but she hoped so.

# Chapter Fifteen

It was four o'clock by the time they got back to Austin's place. The Kellys had been thrilled to hear about the price drop on the house on East Shore, and after they'd gone back to look at it again, Austin had taken them back to the office to write up an offer. He'd been aware of the afternoon ticking away from him, but there was no way he would have made them wait until Monday.

Amber gave him a worried look as he brought the car to a stop. "Are you sure you want me to be here?"

"Of course! What makes you think I wouldn't?"

She looked uncomfortable. "You still have work to do, don't you?"

"No. I took care of it. That's why I took so long. I'm sorry."

"I'm not complaining. I just don't want to mess you up— keep you away from what you need to do."

He smiled and reached across to take hold of her hand. "I've done what I need to do. I'm sorry I was quiet on the way back here. I was running it all through in my mind, making sure I hadn't missed anything." He smiled. "If you want to know the truth, I was distracted all afternoon, thinking about you, looking forward to …" He almost said tonight, and that wouldn't have been a lie, but it might give her the wrong idea, and it wasn't the whole truth. "… looking forward to being with you again, and to seeing where we can go, now that you've told your parents."

She smiled. "Is it wrong that I feel relaxed and happy, even though I've lied to them?"

He pursed his lips. The answer to that should be yes, but it didn't feel that way. "I think the relaxed and happy comes from being honest with them—about you staying here and about not wanting to get back with Milo."

"Yeah. You're right."

They both looked up at the sound of a vehicle approaching. Austin got out when he saw Dallas's Jeep come around the corner. Amber got out and came around to join him.

Dallas jumped out and grinned at them. "Hey, guys. Sorry. I won't be long. I just need to pick up some of my stuff."

"Where are you going?" Austin had an uneasy feeling he might know where.

Dallas winked at him. "That's none of your business. All you need to know is that I'm getting my stuff and getting my ass out of here, so that you guys can have some peace and quiet."

Austin ran up the steps and let Roscoe out when he saw him bouncing up and down behind the door. "Come on, fella. I didn't mean to leave you this long."

Roscoe jumped around him and then moved on to Amber. He did his now customary move of sticking his nose up her skirt. At least she laughed and bent down to make a fuss over him.

Dallas caught Austin's eye. "I was going to ask if you want me to take Roscoe with me."

Amber straightened up. "No." She glanced at Austin. "Sorry. I don't know what you two are thinking but I've been looking forward to seeing more of my buddy here."

Roscoe stuck his nose straight back up her skirt when she stood up.

Dallas laughed. "What worries me is that he's hoping to see more of you, too."

Amber's cheeks tinged with pink.

"It's okay," said Austin. "I appreciate the offer, but we're just going to hang out here. I've left him by himself a lot this week. I want to get some time with him."

"No problem," said Dallas. "I'll just run up and get my stuff."

"Did you decide on a place?" asked Austin.

The way Dallas smiled told him this wasn't about moving into an apartment. Sure, he was getting out of the way to let Austin get some time alone with Amber, but that look said he was after getting some time alone with a woman, too.

"I did," was all he said.

Austin couldn't help but think that giving Crystal the afternoon off hadn't been the best idea. He'd put money on the fact that Dallas would be spending at least the night at her place.

"Problem?" asked Dallas.

"You tell me."

Dallas grinned. "There won't be. I promise. From what I hear, I even have your blessing."

Austin pursed his lips. He supposed he kind of had given him and Crystal the green light in his conversation with her this afternoon.

He shrugged. "I am not my brother's keeper."

Dallas laughed. "That's right. Live and let live. I'm getting out of your hair. You stay out of mine."

After he'd gone, Austin looked at Amber. "Well, that wasn't too subtle, was it?"

She smiled. "After telling my family that we're engaged, I can hardly complain when yours makes it obvious that he's clearing out so we can be alone together."

He smiled and went to her. "You won't hear me complaining."

Her tongue darted out to moisten her lips. "Or me."

He slid his arms around her waist and drew her against him. "So, we have the place to ourselves for the rest of the weekend. What do you want to do?"

She pressed herself against him, and for a moment he thought she was about to suggest that they take it upstairs. He should have known better. She might want to, but she wasn't the kind of girl who'd say so.

She smiled. "I brought my swimsuit."

He nodded. It was hot, and he wouldn't mind a swim himself. He looked down at Roscoe who was watching them and panting. He'd no doubt have fun in the pool, too. And besides, he'd love to see Amber in a swimsuit—especially if he got to take it off her later.

"Do you want to get changed, then? I'll fix us some drinks and see you out there."

"Okay. I'll just get my bag."

He'd forgotten that her bag was still in the SUV. He went with her to get it and took it upstairs for her. She carried on toward the spare room she'd slept in last night, but he stopped at his bedroom door and raised an eyebrow at her.

Her tongue darted out and ran over her bottom lip again, making him want to take her into the bedroom and forget about swimming.

There was hesitation in her eyes when she met his gaze.

"It's okay if you don't want to."

She shook her head rapidly and came back to him. "I do want to."

He set her bag down on the bed and closed his arms around her. "You have to take the lead, Amber."

She leaned back to look up into his eyes. "What do you mean?"

"I mean, you already know what I want. I'm going to leave the rest up to you. I already know you well enough to know that you like to make people happy—you're a pleaser. I don't want you doing anything just to please me."

She reached up and landed a peck on his lips. "You told me that I'm sweet-natured, but I hope you know that you are, too?"

He shrugged. "I just ... I don't want ..." He didn't know how to explain to her that he hated feeling that she'd been with someone who took advantage of her. He didn't expect anything of her.

"I know. And I love that about you."

His heart pounded in his chest. For one crazy moment, he'd thought she was about to say that she loved him. The craziest thing about it was that he wanted to say it back.

He let go of her and stepped away. He needed to put a lid on that! Here he was saying that he didn't want to pressure her into anything. How much pressure would she feel if he told her that he loved her? And where had that even come from? The L word had nothing to do with it … yet.

"I'll go and fix those drinks."

Amber felt self-conscious when she came downstairs. She also wanted to strangle her sister. She'd put her one-piece suit into her overnight bag—the safe one, the one that covered everything and was better suited to swimming laps than lounging by the pool. Jade must have made a switch on her. The bikini she was wearing left nothing to the imagination. Amber had never even seen it before. She'd had to smile when she looked herself over in the mirror. There was no denying that it made the most of her figure.

She took a deep breath and let it out slowly before she slid open the patio door and went out onto the deck.

Austin was sitting on one of the loungers. Her heart beat faster at the sight of him. She was glad that she'd already seen his bare chest this morning. It had taken her breath away then. Now it did so again. He was lean and muscular. He was wearing swim shorts, but her body reacted to him as if he were wearing just underwear—ready for her.

He looked and smiled when he saw her. She stood still as he let his gaze travel over her. Her body reacted as if it were a caress. Shivers ran down her spine and goosebumps covered her arms. She wanted to hug herself to cover her nipples which tightened, and to her embarrassment, pointed straight at him.

She forced herself to smile back at him.

He shifted on the lounger and gestured for her to join him on the other one.

She sat down and hugged her knees to her chest, hoping to cover up the most obvious signs of her attraction to him.

He held her gaze for a moment. "Wow!"

She chuckled. "Thank you, and ditto."

He smiled and leaned forward. "I want to act all cool and confident here, but that's not who I am, and you know it. He folded his arms and rested them on his knees. I think I'm better off admitting the effect you have on me than trying to hide it."

She gave him a puzzled look, and he chuckled and looked down at his lap. "I'm very pleased to see you."

She glanced at his shorts and understood immediately. "Oh!" her heart raced to think that she could have that effect on him. She laughed. "Well, just so you know." She let go of her knees and leaned forward so he could see her chest. Then dropped her gaze toward the two embarrassing peaks sticking through the thin fabric of her bikini top. "I'm pleased to see you, too."

She drew in a sharp breath as he looked, and his eyes darkened. The green and gold shimmer turned a deep shade of green as he looked at her breasts.

When he dragged his gaze away, he looked up into her eyes. "It's mutual, then?"

She nodded eagerly. "Very."

"I wouldn't want you to go along with anything just to please me."

She felt her cheeks color, but she had to say it. She needed him to know what she wanted—that she wanted him. "I'm looking forward to pleasing you."

"Damn!" he breathed. His expression looked almost pained. For a moment she thought she'd done wrong, but he smiled and patted the space between his legs. "Perhaps you'd better come sit here, then. Because I'm not sure I can wait to please you."

She had to swallow as she sat between his legs and leaned back against him. One arm slid around her waist and the other brushed her hair away from her neck. His warm soft lips brushed over her skin and she couldn't help but let out a low moan.

"Oh, God, Austin, that feels so good."

"I want to make you feel good."

She wriggled her backside against him. She could feel how hot and hard he was as he pressed against her. "We could swim later," she suggested.

"I think we should."

She bit down on her bottom lip as his fingers found their way inside the bikini top and circled her nipple. She closed her eyes to enjoy the sensation, then opened them again in a hurry when his other hand slid inside the bikini bottoms. She moaned as he traced her entrance.

"I want you, Austin."

He nibbled her neck and made her shudder. "I want you, Amber."

She turned to look into his eyes. "Do you want to take it inside?"

Her tummy flipped over when he smiled and shook his head. "I'd rather take you right here."

The surprise in her eyes when he said that, made him even harder for her. She wanted him. Everything about her confirmed it, but she was shocked that he would want to do it here. He brushed his lips over hers and then looked down into her eyes.

She nodded. Her breath was coming slow and shallow, and he couldn't help but watch her breasts rise and fall. He unhooked the bikini and sucked in a sharp breath when it fell to her lap. He filled his hands with her plump breasts, and closed his eyes as she wriggled against him, her ass tormenting his cock as she pressed back on him.

He wanted to take his time and get to know her body. He teased her stiff nipples between his fingers and thumbs and then dipped his hand back between her legs. She was hot and wet as he stroked her. She squirmed against him again, and he couldn't take any more. Sitting behind her like this wasn't going to allow him to do all that he wanted to. He shifted so that he was sitting beside her and claimed her mouth. He kissed her more deeply than he'd allowed himself to until now. Her hands came up around his shoulders, and she clung to him as he lay her down. He got rid of his shorts and her bikini bottoms and then sat back to drink in the sight of her. She was beautiful.

She held her arms up to him. How was he supposed to say no to that? He lowered himself to lie beside her, but she made a needy little moan and pulled him closer, working her way underneath him. He positioned himself above her and looked down into her eyes. The way she smiled at him filled his chest with warmth.

"I feel like you want to do all kinds of things to me, and I have no doubt that they would feel so good." She stopped and he could see her swallow before she continued. "I hope that we'll get to them later, but right now, Austin ..." She swallowed again. "Right now, I want you to ... I need ..." Her fingers closed around him and her eyelids drooped. "I want to feel you inside me."

How was he supposed to say no to that? Why would he want to?

He nodded and spread her legs with his knees. He closed his eyes when he pressed into her wetness. He wanted to take his time, make her feel good. She surprised him when she lifted her hips. They both gasped as he dipped inside her.

Her arms tightened around his shoulders. He clenched his jaw as she nibbled his collar bone and breathed, "Please, Austin."

He thrust hard. He had no choice.

She let out a little yelp that only spurred him on. She felt so damned good. So wet and so tight. Her body moved with him as he lost himself inside her. He caught her mouth in a kiss. His tongue mirrored the movements of his cock, thrusting deep inside her, plundering her as she gave herself up to him. She brought out something in him—a need to become a part of her, to fill her with pleasure, as he took his own pleasure in her. She was taking him to the edge, and there was nothing he could do but make sure he took her with him.

She tightened around him with every thrust of his hips. She clenched him tighter and tighter as her gasps became moans. All the pressure that had been building inside him spilled over when she gasped his name. "Austin! Oh, God! Austin. Yes!"

Her body trembled under him and pulsated around him as he let himself go. Waves of pleasure rushed through him, flowing into her as she clung to him. Their bodies frantically melded into one, until they finally lay still.

He rested his head on her shoulder and tangled his fingers in her hair. If he'd thought he was in love with her before, he knew he was lost now. He turned and kissed her cheek.

"Damn, Amber!"

Her body quivered when she chuckled. "If what we just did means I'm damned, then I hope I'm damned for all eternity."

His heart felt like it might have exploded in his chest when she said that. He couldn't help the smile that spread across his face, but then he got a grip. She didn't mean it like that. Just because he'd gotten carried away and somehow fallen for her, it didn't mean that she felt the same way—not yet. All eternity was just an expression.

She gave him a puzzled look. "Are you okay?"

He nodded and brushed the hair away from her forehead. "More than okay. I was just contemplating the possibility of all eternity with you."

Her eyes widened. For a moment he'd swear that she felt it, too, but then she smiled. "That'd be a lot of sex."

He frowned. He wasn't just talking about sex. She was though, and he could hardly blame her. As far as she knew, they were just joking around.

# Chapter Sixteen

When Amber woke on Sunday morning, it took her a moment to figure out where she was. It came back to her when she started to move, and Austin's arm tightened around her middle. She smiled and relaxed back against him, then shivered when his warm lips kissed the back of her neck. Her body woke up in a hurry. Memories of yesterday and last night flooded her with heat.

"G'morning," he breathed.

"Good morning."

She turned over to face him. He was so gorgeous. She couldn't believe how lucky she was to be here in his bed.

He smiled and dropped a kiss on her lips. "I've been thinking."

"What about?" The way he smiled made her guess that it was about something they could do together—here in bed. He'd already proven to her that he had some good ideas about that. Well, to be fair, not necessarily in bed. So far, they'd also made the most of the sun lounger, the sofa and … the kitchen table.

He dropped a kiss on her lips and held her closer to him. She loved the way his hard chest felt against her breasts—and the way his hard cock felt against her stomach. "I've been thinking that Jade may have been right when she said you should stay here for the week."

Amber's smile faded as she remembered why Jade had suggested that. It was to help them convince her parents—help them pull off the lie that they were engaged.

Austin's smile disappeared. "Unless, of course, you don't want to."

"No!" She wrapped her arms around him and held him closer. "You must know that I want to—that I'd love to, but …" She hesitated. She wanted to tell him, but … No. She couldn't hide it. She was just going to tell him. She met his gaze. "When you mentioned Jade, it reminded me that this is only for my parents' sake. To make them believe the lie that we're engaged. It's just for a minute there … God, I hope this doesn't freak you out, but I have to be honest with you. I wished … I wished it was for real."

His expression softened and he dropped a kiss on her lips. "I do, too. I want it to be for real, Amber."

Her heart raced in her chest.

"So, why don't we make it real? Stay here with me—because you want to, because I want you to."

She nodded slowly. "Do you really?"

"I don't think I've ever wanted anything more in my life."

She wanted to melt into him when he claimed her mouth in one of those kisses. She got lost in it, got lost in him. He was so gentle and yet so strong. She stroked his shoulders and rubbed her hips against him, hoping that they might start today the same way they'd ended yesterday.

All of a sudden, the bed started to move. She couldn't understand what he was doing, it was as if he was making love to her, but he was lying still. He broke the kiss and turned to look over his shoulder.

"Roscoe! Get off me, you old perv!"

The bed stilled and Roscoe stepped over Austin and lay down in between them. He licked Austin's face and then turned to lick Amber's. She laughed and pushed him away. Unfortunately, once he got up, he mounted her leg and started humping her through the covers.

"Roscoe!" Austin swatted his ass. "Stop it! I'll put you out and close the door."

Roscoe panted at him and then half-heartedly humped her leg again before jumping down from the bed.

Austin gave her a rueful smile. "Sorry about that."

She laughed. "It's okay. I'm flattered that he likes me. Lenny says he's not always friendly with people."

Austin laughed. "Lenny's being kind. Most people think he's a menace. That's why I don't bring him into town with me much."

"Aww." Amber turned to look at him. "He's a big softie."

"He is, but he's also a bit too protective of me."

"Oh. I didn't think about that. I'm lucky he likes me then."

The way Austin smiled at her melted her heart. "He's a smart dog. I think he knows that I don't need protecting from you. What I need is all the help I can get to encourage you to stick around."

"Aww." She planted a kiss on his lips. "I've already told you. I want to stay the week."

He nodded. "And what about after—"

Roscoe cut him off when he let out a loud bark and ran out of the room. Amber could hear him racing down the stairs barking all the way. She looked at Austin, but he was already out of bed, pulling his sweatpants on.

"I'd better go see what it is."

Amber watched him go and then lay back on the pillows. Had he really been about to ask her if she wanted to stay here even after next weekend—after her parents had been and gone? She smiled to herself. She'd love to! But perhaps that wasn't what he'd meant at all? Perhaps she was just getting carried away.

He was so wonderful, and she was so caught up in him, it'd be easy to get carried away, to start believing that this was for real. She gave herself a shake and got out of bed. It was bad enough that she'd roped the poor guy into being her pretend fiancé; she didn't need to go putting him under pressure by letting him know that she wished it wasn't just pretend.

~ ~ ~

Austin dived into the pool and swam the length of it before he surfaced. The water felt good. He needed something to cool him off—both physically and emotionally. He'd been about to ask Amber why she didn't just stay with him—even after her parents' visit. Perhaps he'd been right about how smart Roscoe was in protecting him. The damn dog had run off barking, just like he did whenever anyone came to the house, but when Austin had followed, there hadn't been anyone there. He'd just saved Austin from making a fool of himself.

Would he want her to stay here with him? He knew the answer as he made the turn and dived back under the water. Yes. He did want her to. He already knew it, but he also knew it was too soon to ask her. He should wait. He should see what she even wanted to do after her parents had been and gone.

When he reached the other end of the pool, he hauled himself up onto the side and sat there enjoying the warmth of the sun beating down on his shoulders.

"You swim like a professional." He couldn't take his eyes off her in that bikini. That was part of the reason that he'd made himself dive in in the first place. All he wanted to do was undress her and make love to her again.

He smiled. "I used to compete as a kid."

She nodded. "I should have guessed."

She came and sat down beside him and dangled her legs in the water. He slung his arm around her shoulders.

"What were you like as a kid? What were you into?"

She looked up into his eyes, and he had to drop a kiss on her lips. She smiled. "I was a good girl. I bet you could have guessed that, too."

He nodded. "Yeah. You don't surprise me."

"I was always in Jade's shadow."

He frowned. He could see it, but he didn't like the idea of it.

She shrugged. "She's more outgoing than I am. More confident." She smiled. "More opinionated. She always needs people to know that's she's there and to know what she thinks. I'm not like that. I just want everyone to be happy."

He tightened his arm around her shoulders. "I think we're all alike in that. I like to keep everyone happy, to make sure everyone's taken care of. There's one big difference between us, though."

She looked up into his eyes. "What's that?"

He smiled. "I make sure I include myself. I make sure I take care of me and make myself happy. You put yourself last."

She opened her mouth as if to protest, and then nodded slowly. "I suppose. I don't mean to. It's not some intentional self-sacrifice. I just ... I get so focused on making sure everyone else is okay, that I don't even notice until it's too late that I've messed myself up."

He nodded. He guessed that she was talking about Milo and her parents, but he didn't want to ask. Didn't want to take the conversation back to that. He'd rather talk about the two of them—and the future, than about her and her ex and the past.

She gave him a puzzled look. "Do you mind if I ask you something?"

"Anything you like."

She blew out a sigh. "I don't really like, but I want to know. About you and Nadia. Were you ... was that about making yourself happy?"

His heart sank. He hadn't wanted to talk about her ex, he certainly didn't want to talk about his. He wasn't going to avoid it, though.

"It was about making myself happy in the beginning. I was flattered that she was interested in me." He wondered how that must sound, but it didn't matter. "When we first started dating, she'd just come back from college. You know she's a lawyer?"

Amber nodded.

"That's how I got to know her. She was representing the family in a probate case. She was very focused on work and success." He shrugged. "It took me too long to learn that her interest in me was mostly about work and success. She thought I was a good prospect." He shrugged. "She's ..." He hesitated. He didn't want to talk badly about her, but he couldn't think of anything good to say. "Do you even want to know?"

Amber nodded. "If you don't mind telling me? I want to understand who you are ... and how you see relationships. For the first few months I was here, you were still with her." She smiled. "And I was jealous."

That sent a jolt through him. He loved thinking that she'd liked him from afar, just as he'd liked her—even though he was still with Nadia.

"It never seemed like you were happy with her though. And none of your friends seemed to like her. I just couldn't work it out. I still can't."

He nodded. "Okay. We were together for a long time. In the beginning, like I said, I was flattered that she was interested in me. Over time, I learned that we didn't have the same values. But she thought she could mold me into the kind of man she wanted, and I guess, if I'm honest, I thought I should let her— that she'd somehow make me a better man if I let her." He shrugged. "I was wrong about that. I couldn't be, wouldn't want to be the kind of man she wants. I tried for a while. Then I said that maybe it'd be better if we went our separate ways, but she asked if we could try. So, we did. We'd become a habit for each other. She got into the habit of feeling disappointed in me, and I got into the habit of trying to do and be what she wanted."

"That's sad. What made you finally break the habit?"

He thought back to the night he'd finally told Nadia it was over. "It wasn't just one thing. It was the realization that as long as we stayed together, I'd always feel like I was a disappointment. Like I couldn't do anything right." He caught her gaze. "And I have to be honest, ever since we met, I couldn't help wondering what it'd be like if …"

She reached up and touched his cheek. "I felt so bad wondering about you. You were still with her, and for all I knew you were going to get married."

He frowned. "What makes you say that?"

"That's what her friends said. I think they knew I liked you. They sat next to Jade and me at the bar one night and talked about how she was just waiting for you to pop the question."

Austin blew out a sigh. "I never planned to do that. Never."

She rested her head against his shoulder. "You poor thing. You went from a girl who expected you to propose to her, to one who just went ahead and told her parents that you had. And you never planned to ask anyone."

He tightened his arm around her shoulders. She'd misunderstood him, and he needed her to know. "No. I meant I'd never planned to ask Nadia."

She looked up into his eyes.

"I do want to propose to the girl I love one day." It was safe to say it because she didn't know yet that she was the girl he loved.

She smiled. "That's good. You're the kind of guy who should be married."

He nodded. He thought so, too.

The day flew by. Amber was shocked when she noticed the time. If she was going to go home, she should go soon. She didn't want to, but after their conversation earlier, perhaps it was best. She was feeling even worse now about roping him into this lie for her parents.

She'd meant it when she said that he was the kind of guy who should be married. He was. He was caring and kind. He'd agreed with her, too—and talked about wanting to ask the girl he was in love with to marry him. She sighed. That was one lucky girl. Whoever she was, whenever she came along, Amber wanted to envy her, but she couldn't help but like her. She'd have to be someone special for Austin to fall for her. He was one special guy.

He came back outside to where she was sitting by the pool and dropped a kiss on her lips. "I haven't wanted to say anything. I wanted to make today last, and just enjoy it for what it is, but …"

She sighed. "I was doing the same, but …" She gave him a sad smile. "It's time for me to go, right?"

He pursed his lips. "If you want to. I'll take you. I was hoping you might want to stay, but …"

"I'll stay then."

"I don't want you to do it for me."

She laughed. "What makes you think that?"

"You just said it was time for you to go."

"Only because I thought that was what you were going to say. I didn't want to make it hard for you to kick me out."

He took her hand and pulled her to her feet. When she stood, he closed his arms around her and held her close. She could feel his heart pounding in his chest.

"I think we need to get something straight, Amber. I haven't wanted to say too much because I don't want you to feel pressured. I don't want you to feel like you just escaped Milo only to be landed with another guy who's trying to claim you. But I need you to know. I want this. I want you. I want you to be my girl for my sake and for your sake, not just because you told your parents you were engaged, but because you want to be with me." He smiled. "Even if it's only half as much as I want to be with you."

Her heart was thundering in her ears now. "You do?"

He nodded. "More than anything."

She couldn't help the smile that spread across her face. "I don't think I want to be with you half as much as you want to be with me."

His arms tightened around her and lines of disappointment etched his face.

"Don't look like that! I don't mean it that way. I mean I think I want to be with you twice as much as you want to be with me."

A look of relief washed over him. "I doubt that's true. There's something else I should tell you."

"What?"

He shook his head slowly. "It's not the right time yet. After your parents have been here and gone. Ask me then."

"Are you sure you don't want to tell me now?"

He smiled. "I want to, but it's better if I wait."

"Okay. I trust you."

"Thank you. That means more than you know. Do you trust me enough not to wear you out this week?"

She raised an eyebrow at him.

"What I'd like to do is take you back to your place so you can get your things, then bring you back here ..." He let his gaze travel over her, sending shivers racing through her. "To bed. Then I'd like you to stay for the week, get to know each other properly—in every sense. Then when we have your parents over next weekend, they won't be able to doubt." He bit his lip and held her gaze for a long moment before he added. "And after they leave, you won't be able to doubt that I want you to stay."

Wow! She'd thought that was what he meant this morning. Now he was saying it again. She slid her arms up around his shoulders and reached up to kiss him. His arm tightened around her and the other came up as he tangled his fingers in her hair. He pulled her head back to give himself better access as he deepened the kiss and left her sagging against him, clinging to him in an attempt to stay upright, even though she'd rather be horizontal with him at this point.

When he finally lifted his head, he looked down into her eyes. She smiled and nipped his bottom lip. "You told me I should put more effort into doing things that make me happy. So, I'm going to do just that. Everything you just said would make me very happy indeed. So, I'm not going to doubt or question. I'm just going to say, yes. Let's go to my place and get some more of my things so I can spend the week here with you."

Her chest filled with warmth when he smiled. "Let's get lots of your things, huh? Much more than you'll need for just the week."

# Chapter Seventeen

Austin was surprised to find the office unlocked when he got there on Monday morning.

"Crystal?"

"Oh. Hey!" Sounds of movement came from her office and then she popped her head out. "I didn't expect you yet. I'll be right out."

He frowned to himself as he went through to the back to start the coffee. She wasn't usually here before him. And despite having lingered in bed with Amber this morning, he wasn't late.

She came out a few minutes later and gave him an odd look. "How was the rest of your weekend?"

He couldn't help smiling. "It was great." He was looking forward to the rest of the week being just as good, too. The day hadn't even started yet, and he couldn't wait to go home this evening and have dinner with Amber, hang out with her, and then go to bed with her again tonight. He had to reel his mind back in, had to come back to today and the work he had to do. And perhaps he should be more curious about what was going on with Crystal.

"Are you okay?" he asked. She was fiddling with her blouse, trying to straighten it.

"Never mind changing the subject. I want to know more about just how great your weekend was."

He turned to see Dallas standing in the doorway. It was weird that he hadn't heard him come in.

Dallas grinned at him. "Let me guess, you and Amber never set foot outside the bedroom after I saw you guys?"

Austin made a face at him. He didn't want to talk about that in front of Crystal.

Dallas laughed. "Sorry, I didn't mean to put you on the spot. Just tell me that she stayed?"

He nodded.

"Awesome. And is she going to come back and stay next weekend, too?"

Austin glanced at Crystal. There was no harm in her knowing. He shook his head.

Dallas's smile faded. "No?"

"No. She's not coming back next weekend. She's staying."

"Wow!" Dallas raised an eyebrow at him. "Like, permanently?"

"I hope so. Anyway, let's get a coffee and you can come in with me. There's a lot we need to go through before I can let you loose around here."

Once they were settled in his office, Dallas grinned at him. "Have you asked her to move in with you already? I know you're a one-woman kind of man, but isn't this a bit fast, even for you?"

Austin shrugged. "It's not like that. Not really."

"What is it like then?"

Austin knew he should tell him about her parents and about Milo, but he didn't know what he'd think.

"Tell me?"

He blew out a sigh and told him all about what Jade had done, about Milo's phone call and everything, right up to him telling Amber that he'd like her to stay even after her parents came to visit.

When he'd finished, Dallas sat back in his chair and sipped his coffee.

"Say something?"

Dallas chuckled. "I'm not sure I know what to say to that, A."

"Do you think I'm crazy?"

"I should. But I don't. I'm surprised at you for going along with a lie, but then, even that. I can see why you're doing it. Especially after her ex called you like that. But where's it all going?"

Austin shrugged. "I told you. I ... I'm falling for her." He didn't want to go as far as to admit that he already had.

Dallas smiled. "Fallen, not falling. Even I can see that."

Austin nodded. He might not want to admit it, but he wasn't going to deny it.

"That's kind of what I mean. If you want her to stay with you even after you put on the big show for her parents ... that means you want this to be something real."

"I do."

"So ..." He shook his head. "I don't know. Where's it going? Is the pretend engagement just a precursor to the real one?"

Austin dropped his gaze.

"It is, isn't it?"

"It's too soon for that, don't you think?" He expected Dallas to laugh and tell him that hell, yes, it was.

Instead, Dallas shrugged. "Is it? I'm no expert, but I would have thought that once you know, you know. More time isn't going to make any difference. Isn't going to change the way you feel."

"I don't mean that. I know how I feel. I mean Amber needs more time to know how she feels."

"Does she?"

Austin met his gaze.

"Think about it. She strikes me as being a lot like you. I know it was her sister who came up with the lie. But do you think she'd go along with it if she was totally against the idea? I'd bet that she wouldn't, couldn't even consider the idea of pretending to be engaged to someone she wouldn't want to be engaged to."

Austin smiled as he thought about it. "I think you might have a point there. I keep holding back, not wanting to push her, but whenever I let her know how I feel, she's right there with me."

Dallas smiled. "If I had to guess, I'd say that she'd be right there with you all the way to wherever you want to take this." He laughed. "And for what it's worth, I wouldn't mind having her as a sister-in-law. I like her. I mean, after Nadia, anyone would be an improvement. You had me worried for a while that I was going to have to call her family."

"No. I was never going to marry her."

"See that just tells me that you know your own mind. You were with her for years, but you never wanted to marry her. You've only been with Amber for weeks, but you do want to … don't you?"

Austin nodded slowly. "I feel crazy even admitting it, but yeah. I do. We've not been seeing each other long—not long at all, but I've known her for a while, and I've known ever since the day I met her that I wanted to be with her."

"Then I say, go for it."

"There's no rush, is there? She's going to stay with me for the week, so that she ... so that we feel at ease with each other. So that we can pull off being an engaged couple."

"Does she plan to leave after their visit?"

"I already told her that I'd like her stay."

"And she said yes?"

"She didn't say no."

"Then I guess, by then, you'll know if you're going to be an engaged couple—for real."

Austin couldn't help smiling.

~ ~ ~

Lenny raised an eyebrow at Amber when she got to the post office. "Is your sister not coming today?"

Amber bit her bottom lip. She didn't know how to tell her that she didn't know. She hadn't seen her yet this morning, since she'd stayed at Austin's last night.

Lenny figured it out for herself quickly enough. She smiled. "Ah. You're coming from Austin's not from the apartment?"

She nodded.

Lenny smiled. "Well, that's wonderful news. Tell me all about it?"

Amber shrugged. "He agreed to go along with the whole being engaged thing."

"I know that much. And it doesn't explain why you stayed with him last night."

Amber could feel the heat in her cheeks. "I don't suppose it does, does it? He asked me to stay with him."

Lenny's smile faded. "And did you stay because you wanted to or because you wanted to get your stories straight before the weekend."

"I thought at first that it was about getting our stories straight. That was what Jade suggested. But ..." She looked up at Lenny from under her eyebrows. "It's about more than that. I like him a lot."

Lenny grinned. "And he likes you. You should make the most of this week."

"I plan to."

They both looked up when Jade came in. "Sorry I'm a bit late."

"You're not," said Lenny. "And you know, if you don't want to be here, you don't have to."

Jade shrugged. "I like hanging out with you both."

Lenny laughed. "I know, but I don't need you both."

"Are you telling me my services are no longer required?"

"I guess I am."

Amber gave her sister a worried look, but Jade just laughed. "In that case, I might get out of here."

"You can have the job if you want it." Amber spoke before she knew what she was saying.

Her sister and her grandmother both looked at her.

"Would you quit with that?" said Jade. "This is what gets you into trouble. This job makes perfect sense for you. I don't need it." She smiled at Lenny. "I'm not even very good at it. Why would you give it away?"

Amber blew out a sigh. "I'm sorry. I know you're right. But I hate the thought of you not having a job."

"But it'd be okay to leave yourself without one?" asked Lenny. "Even though you're the one who wants to stay here."

Amber shrugged. "I don't know. I need to get over that, don't I?"

They both nodded at her. "You really do."

"You need to start putting yourself first, sis. Like I told you. Figure out what you want and go for it. Let other people fall into place around you. If they can't, that's their problem, not yours." Jade smiled. "You're doing great here. I told you Milo had stolen your shine. But lately, you've gotten it back. Between working here and seeing Austin. You're happy. Don't give that up; don't give it away."

"I know you're right. I am happy. But I want you to be happy, too."

Jade laughed. "And what makes you think that working here would make me happy?"

Lenny laughed with her. "Or me?"

"I just ... I want to make sure you're taken care of."

"I know. But I can take care of myself. You should focus on taking care of yourself." Jade smiled. "Or maybe letting Austin take care of you. Did she tell you that she's staying with him for the week, Lenny?"

"She did." Lenny smiled. "And my guess is that it won't just be for the week."

Amber dropped her gaze. She wasn't ready to tell them that Austin had already talked about her staying after her parents visit.

Lenny patted her arm. "Either you don't know it or you're not ready to admit it. But I think your sister did you a favor."

Amber couldn't help but agree. If it weren't for Jade, she might be back in Bakersfield by now. She might have buckled under Milo's insistence that her parents needed her back. Instead, she was staying with Austin—and wishing that their fake engagement was real.

"What time will you be finished?" Austin couldn't wait to get home and see Amber. He'd left the office early and it occurred to him that she might not be able to do the same.

He could hear the smile in her voice. "We're just closing up now. How about you?"

"I'm done. Do you want to meet me? We could have dinner before we head home?"

"Okay, sure. Where?"

"The Boathouse?"

"Great. I'll be there in a few."

Austin smiled to himself as he walked across the deck of the restaurant. This felt good. It felt right. His stride faltered when he saw Nadia sitting with some of her friends. Luckily, she didn't see him, and he made his way inside. *That*—being with her—had never felt right. There'd been plenty of times when she'd called him and told—told not asked—him to meet her here for dinner after work. In the last couple years, he'd rarely ever made it, whether he was able to or not.

He shook his head. He didn't need to think about that anymore. It'd taken him too long, but he'd ended it. He'd freed himself of her and her expectations and demands. Now, he was with Amber. He knew that she'd never demand anything of him.

"Austin!" He smiled when he saw Kenzie waving at him from behind the bar.

"Hey, Kenzie. Are we still on for tomorrow?"

She grinned. "You bet your ass we are. I'm so excited. You're really going to sell the place to us?"

He nodded happily. He was giving them a great deal on the place, too.

She raised an eyebrow at him. "I know you. We're not a charity case you know. You don't have to feel like you're playing Monopoly with Dallas and you have to help us out."

He had to smile, wondering if she'd somehow managed to read his mind. "I'm happy to help you out."

She frowned. "Just don't screw yourself over in the process?"

"I won't." The way she said it made him think about Amber. He wasn't as bad as her. Yes, he liked to help people, but like he'd told her, he didn't screw himself over. He tried to make sure that everything he did was a win-win for all concerned.

"What are you doing here, anyway? It's not like you on a Monday."

"I'm meeting Amber for dinner."

"Aww. Did you two get together, then? I like her. She's a sweetheart. She's just what you need. Not like *her*." She jerked her head to where Nadia was standing in the doorway that led in from the deck.

Austin blew out a sigh. "She couldn't be more different, I'm happy to say." He just hoped that Nadia hadn't come in to see him. He was relieved when she made her way to the ladies' room.

A few minutes later, Amber appeared in the same spot. The sight of her made his heart race and his palms sweat. He'd never reacted like that to Nadia when they first started seeing each other. He pursed his lips. He had reacted like that toward the end, though—whenever she started to bitch him out.

Amber smiled when she spotted him, and she chased all thoughts of Nadia out of his head.

He got down from his stool and closed his arms around her when she reached him. He dropped a kiss on her lips and smiled. "Hi."

"Hi." Her eyes shone as she smiled back at him.

"What can I get you, sugar?" asked Kenzie. "You guys go grab a table, and I'll bring it over. You want menus, right?"

Amber nodded happily. "Please, Kenzie."

Kenzie laughed. "You two are just adorable together."

"Aren't they?" Austin turned, surprised to see Jade standing behind him. "Have you guys told Kenzie your happy news yet?"

Amber shook her head rapidly and gave Jade a warning look.

They'd talked yesterday about whether they should tell people about the whole engagement thing but hadn't reached a decision. Austin had been relieved that Amber didn't want to lie to everyone. There was no way that she—or he—would tell their friends the same story they were telling her parents. But they hadn't figured out if they wanted to let them in on the lie either.

Kenzie gave them a puzzled look. Austin knew she was sharp, and she confirmed it when she shot a glance at Amber's left hand. "You're not …" She looked up and a mischievous smile crossed her face. "Oh, my God! Are you guys engaged?" She spoke so loudly that a few heads turned in their direction.

Austin's heart sank when he saw that Nadia's was one of them. She was making her way back outside and she stood frozen to the spot glaring at him.

Amber shook her head at Kenzie. "No! That isn't …"

Unfortunately, Jade spotted Nadia at the same time Austin did and she gave her an evil look before turning back to Kenzie and saying in a loud voice. "Aren't they just the perfect couple?"

Nadia turned and stalked back outside.

Kenzie laughed. "Sorry, guys. I couldn't resist. When Jade said you had happy news, that's what I thought she meant. And when I saw that bitch …"

Jade chuckled. "I'm sorry, too. You two are too nice to get it, but it's hard to resist having a dig at someone like her."

Amber shook her head sadly. "I'm not stupid. I understand why you did it. But I wish you hadn't." She looked at Jade. "We hadn't decided what we were going to tell people—or even if we were. Now you can almost guarantee that word will get out."

Kenzie frowned. "I thought I was just messing with her head. Are you saying that you are? That you guys are engaged?" She grinned at Austin. "Damn. You're a dark horse. Way to go!"

He couldn't help smiling, even though he knew he shouldn't. "It's not what you think."

Kenzie's smile faded. "What is it then? You've got me confused."

Amber blew out a sigh. "Jade told my parents that I was engaged to Austin, because she was trying to help me out. They're coming next weekend, and we …" She glanced up at him. "We're going to pretend that we are."

Kenzie gave them a long appraising look. "Hmm. That's a shame."

"What is?" Austin felt bad. It sounded like she was disappointed in him for lying.

She shrugged. "I thought you really were. I should have known though. There's no ring." She smiled at Austin. "And knowing you, it'd be quite a ring."

Austin nodded. If nothing else, this conversation had made him realize that he'd have to do something about a ring before the weekend.

# Chapter Eighteen

Amber smiled when she got out of the car. She could see Roscoe bouncing up and down behind the front door. She hurried up the steps to open it and let him out. He jumped around her a couple of times and then stuck his nose up her skirt.

She laughed and pushed him away. "I can't say we don't know each other well enough for that anymore, but still, you shouldn't do it."

He panted at her and wagged his tail.

"Come on, do you need to take care of business?"

He pricked his ears at that and trotted away to the stand of trees. Amber let out a happy sigh as she watched him. As the week had gone on, she couldn't help wishing that this really was her life. Austin was wonderful. The more time she spent with him, the more wonderful he was. Roscoe was a sweetheart, there was no denying he was a perv, just like Austin called him. But he was affectionate with it. She loved that dog. She looked around. She loved this place. Her heart raced. As much as she tried to avoid facing the thought, she knew that she loved Austin. He was the sweetest, kindest man she'd ever known. She sighed again.

"Come on. Roscoe. Let's get you a walk before Austin gets back."

He came bounding back to her on her full alert, looking around for Austin.

"He'll be here soon."

He had to show a house at five-thirty tonight. He'd told her he'd be back as soon as he could. She planned to make dinner for him. This was the first time she'd been home before him. He'd given her a key on Sunday, so she had no worries about that. It felt strange, though, to be here without him; strange, but good.

She walked up the path that led to the treehouse. Roscoe had been cooped up in the house all afternoon, and she wanted him to get a run. It was always the first thing Austin did when he got home.

When they reached the clearing, she looked up at the treehouse. If she wanted to let herself get carried away she could imagine kids playing up there—her kids, Austin's kids. She felt the heat in her cheeks and looked around. There was no one out here, and they couldn't hear what she was thinking even if there were. But still. It was a ridiculous thing to think— to wish for. He was amazing. But he wasn't really her fiancé.

Her phone rang and she pulled it out of her purse, hoping that it might be him saying he was on his way home already. It wasn't. She didn't recognize the number.

"Hello?"

"Hi, sweetheart."

A shudder ran down her spine at the sound of Milo's voice. She couldn't speak.

"Are you surprised to hear from me?"

"Yes. What do you want?"

"That's no way to talk to me. I want what I've always wanted. I want you."

"It's not going to happen, Milo. We're over. I've told you enough times. And you can't get to me anymore. My parents don't expect me to come home. They know that I'm happy here."

"With your fiancé?" There was an edge to his voice that she didn't like.

"Yes."

"Austin."

"Yes."

"You really think that a guy like that is going to marry you?"

She hesitated for a moment. She wished!

Milo laughed. "There. See. Your silence says it all. You know, don't you?"

"Know what?"

"That you're better off with me. I checked him out. I wanted to make sure you were with someone who'd be good to you."

Amber made a face. As if!

"He's a big deal in that little town where you are. He's not going to settle for someone like you."

Amber frowned. "What do you mean?" Dammit. She shouldn't let him draw her in.

"I mean, a guy with that kind of money isn't going to settle down with a girl like you. You're—"

He was about to put her down. She knew it. "Why do you think we're engaged if he doesn't want to settle down with me?"

Milo laughed. "So, naïve. You're the kind of girl who needs to think it's serious before she'll put out, right? He's just telling you what you want to hear so that he can fuck you. And believe me, he'll only fuck you till he gets bored of you."

Was that really how he thought it worked? "You've got it all wrong, Milo. He's not like you."

"I know. I want more than that from you. I want to marry you."

She laughed. "You don't want me. You don't even mind him *fucking* me. You only want to marry me so that you'll get more control of the business—and so that I'll do more of the work and make your life easier."

Milo was quiet for a long moment. "He told you what I said?"

"Yes, he did! Because he cares about me, and he doesn't lie to me—unlike you."

Milo laughed. "Whatever you say, Amber. Don't worry, though. I'll still take you back when he dumps you."

"He's not going to dump me. He loves me and he's going to marry me! I wish you'd get that through your head and leave me alone." She hit the end call button and stared at the phone. What was his problem? Why wouldn't he just accept that she was done with him? She blew out a sigh and patted Roscoe's head. He'd come to stand beside her while she talked and was leaning against her legs looking up at her.

"It's okay. Don't look at me like that. I'm okay."

Roscoe let out a low whine.

"Honestly." She scratched his ears. "Everything's okay. Come on. Let's go back to the house and start dinner."

~ ~ ~

Austin smiled when he saw Amber's car parked in the garage. He loved the idea that he was coming home to her at the end of the day. He loved the thought that this could really be his life.

He patted his pocket. If she wanted to wear the ring after this weekend, maybe it would be his life. He got out of the SUV and opened the door to the kitchen. The sight of her standing at the stove stirring something made his heart leap into his mouth.

Roscoe let out a happy little yip when he saw him and came running.

"Hey, buddy." He scratched his ears. "I missed you, too." He went to Amber and slid his arms around her waist as she smiled up at him. "Not as much as I missed you, though."

He dropped a kiss on her lips. He only meant it to be a peck, but her arms came up around his neck and she pressed herself against him. His lips crushed against hers and he tasted her, kissing her deeply as he walked her away from the stove and backed her up against the cabinets. He closed his hands around her ass and rocked his hips against hers.

She let out a needy little moan that had him aching for her. He glanced over at the breakfast table and walked her over to it, pushing her skirt up around her waist as they went. She fumbled with his zipper and pushed his pants down.

They'd made a lot of love over the last few days. He'd taken his time getting to know her, learning what pleased her. This time there was an urgency between them. This was about need. He lay her back on the table and hooked his fingers inside her panties, pulling them down and off. He circled her clit with his thumb until she moaned and writhed, and then thrust two fingers deep and hard inside her. She gasped and her eyes widened as they locked with his. He grasped her hips and positioned himself between her legs, then thrust deep and hard. Damn! She felt so good. So hot and wet and tight as she closed around him.

"Austin!"

He smiled as he drove deeper, loving the way his name sounded on her lips. "Do I feel good?"

"Yes! Oh, God! Yes!"

Their bodies melded into one as she moved with him, taking everything he had to give. He tensed as he realized that he wanted to give her everything he had, everything he was.

"Amber!" he gasped as he tensed and let himself go. Waves of pleasure crashed through him, making him see stars as he came hard. She clenched around him, drawing him deeper as they flew away together to a place he'd never been.

When they stilled, he leaned forward, covering her body with his as he kissed her. He lifted his head and looking into her eyes. *I love you, Amber.* The words echoed so loudly in his head that he wondered if he'd said them out loud. Her eyes told him that he hadn't. He wanted to, but he'd decided that he shouldn't, not yet. Not until the weekend and her parents' visit was behind them.

He brushed his hand over her cheek and she smiled.

"Well, I wasn't expecting that."

"I didn't plan it. I couldn't help myself."

Her smile faded. "We're about more than that, though, aren't we?"

He got up and she sat up beside him. "You know we are, don't you? I needed you to know that before we ever went there."

She nodded. "I'm sorry. Of course, I know."

Austin's heart sank. To him, that had been something special. He hated that she thought it was only about the physical.

He put his arm around her shoulders. "I'm sorry."

"No!" She shook her head rapidly and he was stunned to see tears in her eyes.

"What is it? What's wrong?"

She shook her head again. "It's not you. It's … Milo. He called me. I guess I let him get inside my head again."

Austin sighed. "What did he say?"

She shrugged. "He told me that you were only engaged to me because girls like me don't put out unless we think it's going somewhere." She looked up into his eyes. "I know it's stupid. I know you're not engaged to me because you want to sleep with me." She let out a little laugh. "You're not even engaged to me! And you were the one who wouldn't sleep with me unless it meant something, unless it was part of something bigger. It's just …" She looked up into his eyes. "I guess I shouldn't be blaming him. It's me. I … I've been getting carried away with this whole thing. I want it to mean more, to be more. I want …" She shrugged again and looked away. "I think this whole thing has gotten blown out of proportion. I've gotten caught up in wishing it was real, and that's not fair to you. We'd only gone out a few times before this whole engagement thing came up."

He took hold of her hand and squeezed it. "What are you saying?"

"I guess all I'm trying to do is apologize for being so silly. When you came home, and I was here it felt so good, so right. Like this was our life, and I was so lucky to be with you and to have you want me like you did. And then I remembered what Milo said, and it made me feel like I was being stupid because all you were doing, all you wanted to do was come home and find a woman in your kitchen—a woman you could ... fuck."

He sat back at that and shook his head sadly. "You know that's not how I see it."

"I do. And I'm sorry."

His heart was racing. He wanted to kill Milo, but at the same time, a part of him was grateful. He hated that he'd planted doubts in her mind, but he'd also made her come out and admit that she was wishing this was for real—just like Austin was.

"Let's go back a bit?"

She looked up at him. "Where to?"

He smiled. "To the part where you said that this felt good— right—that you were here, and this was our life."

She dropped her gaze. "I'm sorry. I was just getting carried away. You don't need that kind of pressure."

"What if I want it? What if I've been feeling that way, too? Feeling like I'm so lucky to be with you and that you being here feels right?"

Her eyes widened.

"That's how I feel, Amber. Yes, this started out as a lie, but it doesn't feel like one. It feels to me more like we're lying to ourselves than lying to your parents. If Jade hadn't said what she said, I want to think that we would have gotten there anyway."

She bit down on her bottom lip, but it didn't hide her smile. "Do you?"

He nodded. "I do. I don't want this to be about your parents anymore. I want it to be about us and how we really feel."

"I'm not sure I'm ready to tell you how I feel."

His heart slammed to a halt. "Why?"

"Because I don't want to scare you."

He let out a sigh of relief. "Well, I'm sorry if I scare you. But I need you to know." He tucked his fingers under her chin and tilted her head back so she looked up into his eyes. "I love you."

Her eyes filled with tears, and she threw her arms around his neck. "You do?"

He nodded. He knew it was too soon still, but this whole thing had gotten way too complicated, and he needed to take it back to the simple truth.

She planted a kiss on his lips. "I love you, too."

He wanted to be thrilled, but he wasn't entirely sure. "You don't have to say it back just to make me happy, you know."

She gave him a sad smile. "I'm not. I'm saying it because it makes me happy. I didn't want to tell you but … You really do? You love me?"

He chuckled. "I really do. Believe me. I'm not in the habit of saying those three words just because I think someone wants to hear them."

"Well, just so you know, neither am I. In all the time I was with Milo, I never said that."

He tightened his arm around her, not knowing how to tell her how happy that made him.

Roscoe chose that moment to come and start sniffing at Amber's panties.

"Get away, perv!"

Amber laughed and got down from the table. "He kind of has a point. I should probably get cleaned up."

"Yeah." For the first time, it occurred to Austin that they were still sitting on the breakfast table, with their underwear on the floor.

~ ~ ~

After they'd cleaned up. They ate dinner out at the table by the pool. Amber kept glancing at Austin. Her heart felt as though it might overflow. He loved her? He loved her! This wasn't just pretend. It was for real.

He caught her peeking at him and stopped with his fork mid-air and smiled. "What?"

She laughed. "I'm just checking out this hot guy who says he loves me."

He laughed with her. "You can check him out all you like. He's yours."

Her chest filled with that warm feeling. "I can't quite believe it. Don't get me wrong. I want to."

"I understand. I feel the same way. I knew …" He drew in a deep breath. "I know it's fast, but it's not like we got together without knowing each other first. I knew who you were as a person before I ever asked you out." He smirked. "I knew you must have some interest in me too, since you agreed to go out with me even though I made such a mess of asking you."

She smiled. "I didn't think you made a mess of it. I thought I was just such a mess I didn't really understand."

He reached over and squeezed her hand. "I don't think either of us is very good at the whole dating thing, are we?"

She laughed. "I don't mind admitting that I'm not. Look at my track record."

"I'm not saying anything. Mine's no better."

Her heart leaped into her chest when he spoke again.

"I think maybe we should both give up."

"What … what do you mean?"

He smiled. "That I'd like our dating days to be behind us. It's not dating when you live together, is it?"

"Oh! No. I don't suppose it is."

"So, what do you say?"

Her heart was racing. She wanted to be sure that she understood—that he meant what she hoped he did.

He raised an eyebrow. "I know you're living here this week, and I already told you that I'd like you to stay after the weekend. What I'm saying is ... what I'm asking is, do you want to live with me?"

"Yes! I do, Austin. I'd love to."

He leaned across and landed a kiss on her lips. "Thank you."

# Chapter Nineteen

Austin woke early on Saturday morning. He was nervous about this weekend. He hoped that Amber's parents were going to like him. That was important to him, and he knew that he'd gotten off to the wrong start with them. He, personally, hadn't lied to them, but he'd been a part of the lie, gone along with it. And he needed the truth to come out.

Amber rolled over and gave him a sleepy smile. "You're awake, too?"

He dropped a kiss on her lips. "Yup. Good morning."

She made a face. "Do you really think it's good? I'm dreading today."

He nodded. "I can't say I'm thrilled about it."

She sighed. "I'm sorry. I want to say I wish we'd never gone along with this, but I can't because if we hadn't …"

He kissed her again. "Don't say things wouldn't have worked out the way they have between us. It might have taken us a bit longer, but we would have gotten here." He hugged her to his chest. "I honestly believe that we're meant to be."

"Aww." She kissed him. "You're amazing."

He chuckled. "I'm just an ordinary guy."

She laughed out loud at that. "You are so far from ordinary. You're a shining star in a world full of darkness."

He laughed. "I didn't know you were the poetic kind."

She shrugged. "Neither did I, but it's true. You're a star."

"Whatever you say."

"To be fair. It's not what I say. It's what my dad always used to say to Jade and me when we were small. He used to tell us that we were shining stars. I could always see it about Jade. She shines bright in everything. I've never felt like I shine. She's so sweet though. She always tells me that Milo stole my shine."

Austin smiled. "You shine bright to me."

"So, you get it. I don't think I do, but you see it. You don't think you do, but I see it."

Austin nodded. "I like it. It reminds me of a line in a song, something about stars in a sunlit sky. They're still shining, you just don't notice them when it's light."

"Exactly. Most people only pay attention to the sunshine. They don't notice the stars that are still shining quietly in the background."

He hugged her closer. "I love that explanation. We're neither of us people who need to steal the limelight, are we?"

"No. We don't even want it. We can just shine for each other while no one else is looking."

Austin's smile faded. It was all well and good lying here talking about stars, but they were going to have to get up and get on with the day soon.

Amber blew out a sigh. "I wish I hadn't lied to them."

"Maybe it's time to tell them the truth." His heart thundered as he said it, but it was the right thing to do.

She nodded slowly. "I guess there's no reason not to, is there?"

"Not unless you don't want to. Telling them the truth now will mean admitting that we lied before."

"You didn't."

"But I'm in it with you."

"And Jade."

"She already said she doesn't mind admitting it."

Amber nodded. "It's the right thing to do, isn't it?"

"It is. I'd feel better about it."

"Then, that's what we'll do."

Amber looked over at Austin as he drove them into town. "Would you mind if we stop to see Lenny on the way?"

"Of course not."

"Thanks. And do you mind …" She wanted to ask if he minded if she told her grandmother that they were together for real.

He smiled. "You want to tell her that we're not faking it?"

She let out a short laugh. "Yes. It just occurred to me that if I admit that we were lying, it'll mean telling them that she was going along with the lie."

"Ah."

Amber shrugged. "I don't think she'll care, but I'd like to talk to her first."

"I would, too. And did you talk to Jade?"

"Yeah. She's going to meet us later and she doesn't mind at all if we tell them that she made the whole thing up."

Austin frowned.

"I know. I don't want to throw her under the bus. She was only trying to help me out. I'm hoping that I can come clean without making it look like anyone else did anything wrong."

"Hopefully, they'll understand."

"I think they might. Dad was a lot more understanding than I expected when I talked to him last week."

Austin reached over and squeezed her hand. "It'll all be okay. You'll see. And after this weekend we'll be free to get on with our life with none of this hanging over us."

She smiled. That sounded so good.

She paced nervously around the airport building while they waited for the plane to land. She'd only been out here a couple of times when her parents had visited before.

She smiled when she saw Zack come out of the offices in the back. He grinned and came over to them. "Hey guys. It's good to see you. I hear congratulations are in order."

Austin smiled. "Thanks."

"I'm surprised at you, though. I thought you'd have gotten everyone together to tell us yourselves. I was surprised that Nadia of all people was the one sharing your news."

Amber frowned. "What do you mean?"

Zack's smile faded. "Shit! You're not trying to keep it secret, are you? If you are, she's blown it."

Austin blew out a sigh. "Don't tell me. She's going around telling people that we're engaged?"

"Yeah." Zack gave him a worried look. "Is it supposed to be a secret?"

Austin looked at Amber and rolled his eyes. "It's complicated."

"Sorry guys. I won't say another word about it to anyone."

Amber shook her head. "If anyone asks, you should probably tell them it's not true."

Austin gave her a look she couldn't decipher, then turned to Zack. "It's probably better to just play dumb. Don't say anything at all for now."

"Sure." Zack looked out the window as a plane came in to land. "Is that your folks, Amber?"

She nodded. "I think so."

Zack raised an eyebrow. "I guess you don't want them hearing that rumor, if it's not true, huh?"

She had to laugh.

Zack gave her a puzzled look.

"It's like Austin said. It's complicated. Way too complicated."

Austin smiled. "But hopefully, we'll have it all straightened out before the weekend's over."

Zack held his hands up. "I don't get it. I don't think I want to get it. If I can do anything to help, let me know, but other than that, I'm just going to play dumb."

Austin chuckled. "That's probably the best way to go."

"I'll see you around, guys."

Amber looked up at Austin once he'd gone. "Why would Nadia be telling people?"

"She overheard Kenzie the other night when we were at the Boathouse, remember?"

"Oh. But why …?"

Austin shrugged. "I have no idea. And it's not important right now. I'm guessing that's your folks?"

Amber looked to where the doors from the ramp were sliding open. "Yep, that's them."

Austin took hold of her hand. "Are you ready?"

She reached up and kissed his lips. "I am. Are you?"

He smiled. "Yeah. I'm kind of looking forward to it."

She gave him a puzzled look, but there was no time to ask what he meant when her mom spotted them and started waving and hurrying over.

~ ~ ~

Austin took a deep breath and put a smile on his face as they went to meet her parents. Her dad met his gaze with an appraising look. At least it wasn't hostile.

"Mr. Young. It's good to meet you." He held his hand out.

Amber's dad nodded and shook with him. "I'd like to say the same, but I think you'll understand if I reserve judgment on that for a while."

Austin nodded. "Of course." It wasn't as bad as he'd expected.

He turned to her mom, and she smiled. "I'm cautious, too, but …" She smiled at Amber and then back at Austin. "You'll get full points in the first impressions department."

Austin had to smile, though it faded quickly when her dad gave him a stern look.

"I told you, you didn't need to pick us up. I rented a car."

Amber smiled. "I know, but we were excited to see you."

Her dad didn't look convinced. He looked at Austin.

He shrugged and gave him a half smile. He planned to go with the truth whenever possible with them. "I would have used the word nervous, but yeah. We were eager to see you."

"You mean to get this over with?"

Austin met his gaze. He wasn't going to let the man push him around. "More like to get it started so that we can get it straight."

He could feel Amber tense at his side, but to his relief, her dad smiled at him. "Fair enough. We're going to get checked in at the lodge over at Four Mile Creek. Do you want to give me directions to your place and we'll come over when we're ready?"

"I thought we were having lunch with you at the plaza," said Amber.

Her mom smiled. "We thought we'd come and see you first."

"Okay."

Austin nodded. "Do you want me to text you the directions?"

"You can send them to my phone," said her mom. "I'm the navigator."

She told him her number and Austin tapped it into his phone. He sent her the directions and then smiled and took his phone back out. "Actually, I'll give you the code for the gate, too."

Her dad raised an eyebrow. "You live in a gated community?"

Austin had to smile. He usually felt a little bit embarrassed that he'd gone and installed himself a fancy electronic gate, but today he wasn't above using it to try to impress her dad. "No. It's my gate."

Her dad looked a little puzzled, but her mom smiled. "We can't wait to see the place." She touched Austin's arm. "I know you said you're nervous, but there's really no need. All we want is for our little star to be happy."

Amber smiled. "I am."

Her dad met Austin's gaze again. "Of course, we want to get to know you. Make sure that ... that she's okay."

Austin nodded. "I understand. I want you to get to know me. I want you to leave here knowing that she's loved and that she's going to be taken care of."

Amber looked at him, but he continued to meet her dad's gaze.

Eventually, he nodded. "Well, they're bringing our bags out. We'll see you at your place in a while. We'll let you know when we're on the way."

Amber squeezed his hand as they watched her parents follow the guy with bags out to the parking lot.

"I thought we were going to tell them the truth?"

"We are."

"But what you said about me being loved and taken care of ..."

He had to smile, and he dropped a kiss on her lips. "That *is* the truth. We're not trying to convince them about some fake fiancé. I'm letting them know what's really going on."

"Aww." She reached up and planted a kiss on his lips. "You're awesome."

He laughed. "Let's hope we can get them to think that."

~ ~ ~

Amber caught hold of Roscoe's collar when he started to bark. "They must be here."

"Yep."

"Are you okay with all this?"

He smiled. "I am. I'm glad they're here. It's like I told your dad, I want to get this all straightened out."

She raised an eyebrow at him. "What do you mean, exactly?"

The smile he gave her made her insides turn to mush. "I asked you a while ago, if you trust me."

"I do."

"Then trust me on this?"

"Okay."

"Don't worry. I'm going to follow your lead on straightening out all the mess first."

"Thanks. I think I should lead with that, don't you?"

"Yeah. We need to let them know what's really going on. Here, let me get hold of him and you go down to meet them. I think he'll be okay with them."

"You do?"

"Yeah. He's going to have to get used to them."

She didn't get the chance to ask what he meant. Her parents were getting out of the car. Her mom smiled up at them. "This place is wonderful!"

Amber turned back and winked at Austin. She'd known they'd be impressed with the house.

She ran down the steps to meet them and hugged them both. "Come on in. It's a lovely place."

Her dad nodded. "It is." He ran up the steps but stopped a few short of the top when Roscoe started to growl.

"Is he safe?"

Austin looked less confident now than he had earlier. "I'll go and put him in the yard for now, just to be sure."

When he'd gone, Amber's mom turned to her. "Are you sure you're okay with that big dog? He looked dangerous to me."

Amber laughed. 'He's a sweetheart. He's ... oh." It dawned on her. "He's just very protective of Austin. I guess he could sense that you might be a threat to him."

Her dad frowned. "I'm not a threat to him. I just want to know that he's not going to be any kind of threat to you, or your well-being."

"He's not, Dad. He's the best thing that's ever happened to me."

Austin appeared in the doorway at that moment and smiled at her. She wasn't embarrassed; she was glad he'd heard her say that—it was true.

"Come on in," said Austin. "Would you like a drink or do you want to look around the place?"

Her dad went to join him. "I'll take a look around with you while the girls get a drink. Then we can switch."

Amber caught Austin's eye, hoping that he was going to be okay alone with her dad. He smiled and gave her a slight nod. She'd hoped that they might all get together first so that she could tell them the truth about not being engaged. But it could wait a little while longer.

Her mom slipped her arm through hers. "You can get me a drink, but I want to look around while we do. It's a gorgeous place, Amber." She glanced over her shoulder to where the guys were, then grinned. "And don't tell your father, but Austin's gorgeous, too. My goodness! You've not just upgraded from Milo, you've moved into a whole different league."

Amber had to laugh. "That's exactly what Jade said."

Her mom smiled. "Well, Jade would know. She's played in few different leagues herself. Unlike you."

Amber hurried her into the kitchen to get a drink. She didn't want the questions about her and Austin to start too soon. She wanted to tell both of them together.

"Oh, my goodness!" Her mom turned around in a circle. "You know your dad's come looking to find fault with Austin, but once he sees this kitchen, he'll want to move in with you."

Amber had to laugh. "I know. He's going to love it."

Her mom's face sobered. "He will, but the most important question is do you love this Austin? Is he going to be good to you? I never did like you being with Milo."

Amber stared at her. "You didn't? I thought … I thought you liked it … because it was good for the business. Because …"

"To hell with the business. The business is only important because it provides for us—provides for you girls. You're what matters. You and your sister. Whatever makes you happy. And I never thought Milo made you happy. There's something about him … Something shady."

Amber shook her head in wonder. "You're right. There is. He's not a good person. I never wanted to tell you that because …" She shook her head again. "It seems I had everything very wrong. I thought you liked him. I thought you needed him for the business." She blew out a sigh. "I had it all wrong, Mom. I'm sorry. I thought you guys wanted me to come back there and get together with him."

"Hell, no! I was so relieved when you came up here. Don't get me wrong. I was worried about your grandmother. But I hoped you might find a better life here." She smiled and looked around the kitchen again. "It sure looks like you have. You know I want to hear all about how you and Austin got together. How he proposed."

Amber cringed. She knew she needed to tell them the truth sooner than later. "We should see if they're done looking around, and I can tell you both together."

"Okay. But I have to warn you. Your dad was disappointed that Austin didn't ask him first."

Amber nodded. She could hardly explain.

# Chapter Twenty

Austin walked beside Amber's dad out the back. He wasn't anywhere near as bad as Austin had expected him to be.

"So, is this where you grew up? Your family home?"

"No, sir. I grew up in town."

"Where?"

Austin smiled as he realized something. "If I have it right, then about three doors down from where you did."

Amber's dad frowned. "On Sycamore?"

"That's right."

"My mom is Tonya Anderson. Well, she's been Tonya Williams for nearly forty years."

"Jesus! You're Tonya's kid?"

Austin smiled. It'd never occurred to him before that his mom and Amber's dad must have gone to school together. They'd both grown up here and were about the same age. "Yes, sir."

"You might as well call me Bill." He gave Austin a grudging smile. "You seem like you're in a hurry to win me over, and I haven't seen anything so far to tell me that you shouldn't."

Austin relaxed a little. "I'm doing my very best. But I will tell you, I'm not doing anything for your sake. I want you to see and know who I am. I'm not going to try to be or do something just so that you'll like me."

Bill's mouth turned down. "Yeah. I already know that."

"What do you mean?"

"You didn't exactly endear yourself by not asking me first."

"Asking you?"

Bill blew out a sigh. "I'll get over it, but in my book a man would come to his girl's father to ask for his blessing first."

"Ah." Austin's heart sank. He could hardly explain that he felt the same way. Not without …

"What? You look like you have something to tell me?"

He shook his head. He did but he couldn't.

"You wouldn't lie to me would you Austin? We're not going to do very well together if you lie."

Austin blew out a sigh and met Bills gaze. "I want to tell you the truth."

Bill's expression hardened. "What's going on?"

Austin pursed his lips and nodded. He had to explain.

~ ~ ~

"Where do you think they've gotten to?" Amber's mom asked her. "It looks like a big place, but it shouldn't take them this long to do a tour."

Amber wrung her hands together. She was starting to get worried. She wanted to tell her parents the truth. But she needed them both here so she could. And she had no idea why her dad was keeping Austin so long. She hoped he wasn't interrogating him. Poor Austin didn't need that. He was only going through all of this for her.

A wave of relief rushed through her when they appeared outside the patio door. They were smiling—thank goodness. And even better, Roscoe was with them. That must mean he no longer saw her dad as a threat to Austin—that had to be a good sign.

Her mom got down from her seat at the counter and went to open the door. "Where've you been?"

The way her dad smiled made Amber wonder what was going on. "We've just been getting to know each other." To her amazement, he grasped Austin's shoulder. "I like this guy." He nodded at her as if he was letting her know that she had his approval. She relaxed, relieved for a moment, but then she tensed again. They still had to come clean about the fact that they weren't really engaged—that they'd lied!

Her dad took hold of her mom's hand. "You need to come out here a minute, love."

Amber started to follow them. She was surprised that her dad wanted to show her mom something outside rather than come in and see the kitchen.

He waved a hand at her. "You wait there. You can get me a drink if you want. You've seen it all before."

She stopped. Wow. She hoped they weren't getting Austin by himself to warn him off. She'd give them a few minutes but then she'd have to go out there and make sure everything was okay.

"What do you want to drink?" She called after them.

"You got any bubbly?"

Amber made a face. "Prosecco?"

Austin smiled at her. "Don't worry about it. There's some champagne in the fridge in the garage. I'll bring it when we come back in."

"Are you okay?"

He smiled. He didn't seem worried in the least. Either he'd won her dad over, or he wasn't aware what he was in for yet. "I'm great, sweetie. We'll be back in a few minutes."

Amber poured herself a glass of wine. This was too strange for words. She just wanted to get them all in here so that she could tell them the truth.

She sipped her wine and waited as the minutes ticked by. She couldn't take any more. She went to the window, but they weren't out there. She turned at the sound of a car door out front. Who was that? She didn't need anyone else turning up. She just wanted to sit down with Austin and her folks and tell them the truth.

The front door opened, and Jade came in. "Hey, sis!"

"What are you doing here?"

"Is that any way to greet your favorite sister?"

Amber narrowed her eyes at her. "I still haven't had the chance to tell them the truth. I need them to myself. I don't want …"

"Don't want what?" asked her dad. Amber's heart sank when her parents appeared behind Jade.

Then Lenny stepped around them and came to her and took hold of her hands. "It's okay, Amber don't worry."

Her heart was racing now. Austin came in after them and gave her what looked like a reassuring smile. Lenny stepped back and he came and took her hand.

"What's going on?"

"You said you trust me?"

She nodded. "I do, but …" she glanced at her parents.

Her dad smiled. "It's okay, Amber. He explained everything."

Her heart leaped into her mouth and tears pricked behind her eyes as she looked up at Austin.

He put his arm around her shoulders. "Please don't be mad at me. I needed to clear everything up."

She nodded.

"You've been so torn up about it, and you didn't cause any of it. I need you to know that I've got your back. I'll make things better for you wherever I can."

She had to swallow around the lump in her throat. "Thank you."

He hugged her into his side and then led her through to the kitchen. She had to wonder what everyone else was doing here as they followed them.

She stopped dead when she saw Dallas was already in the kitchen. Where on earth had he come from? And an older couple was with him. They had to be Austin's parents; she could tell just by looking at them. She knew she was going to like them, but she couldn't figure out what they were doing here.

"I'd like you to meet my mom and dad."

She stepped forward to shake hands with them, but his mom wrapped her in a hug, then his dad did, too.

"It's lovely to meet you."

"And you. We've heard so much about you."

"You have?" She looked up at Austin. She didn't like to say that she hadn't heard much about them.

Dallas grinned at her and stepped forward to hug her.

Austin chuckled. "Put her down."

Dallas stepped back with a grin and went to stand beside Jade before he said, "Come on Austin, put the poor girl out of her misery. She doesn't have a clue what's going on."

Amber had to laugh. "I don't! I feel like I'm in one of those dreams where everyone knows what's going on except me." She gave Austin a pleading look.

He dropped a kiss on her lips. "Like I said. I straightened things out with your mom and dad." She glanced over at them and they smiled and nodded.

"I wish you felt you could have been honest with us, love," said her dad. "But we understand. And …" He smiled at Austin. "It's all worked out for the best in the end."

Jade grinned at him. "It will, if you'll let him get on with it."

Austin turned back to her and took hold of her hands. "We said we were going to tell them the truth today. And I have. The thing is, I told them a little more of the truth than I've told you."

Her heart started to race. "What do you mean?"

"Nothing bad, sweetie. I promise."

She relaxed a little at that. She did trust him.

"What I've told your folks…" He smiled and looked around at the rest of their family. "… and everyone else here. Is that I love you."

He dropped down on one knee and tears filled her eyes. "I love you and I don't want to be your fake fiancé. I want to be your real one. I know we haven't been together for long, but I also know that you're the person I want to spend the rest of my life with, Amber. I love you. You're the most beautiful person I've ever known—inside and out. I want to spend the rest of my days making you happy. Will you marry me?"

Her heart was thundering in her ears. She couldn't believe this was happening. His eyes looked so serious, shimmering gold and green. He was waiting, he started to look worried.

"Yes! Yes, I'll marry you, Austin. I love you."

He slid a ring on her finger and then stood up and closed his arms around her. She got lost in his kiss. It didn't matter that her parents were right there. Nothing mattered other than this wonderful man—the man who was going to be her husband!

Everyone hugged them and congratulated them. Amber felt as though she was walking on air.

He hugged her to him and dropped a kiss on her lips. "I told you that after this weekend we'd be free to put all that stuff behind us and get on with our life."

She squeezed her arms tight around his middle. "You did. But I had no idea that this is what you meant."

"I had to make it right, Amber. For you and for your folks. For us."

Jade came to join them and handed them each a glass of champagne. "We should drink a toast to the happy couple."

Amber took it from her. "Did you know about this?"

She laughed. "Not a clue until a little while ago when your man here roped me in to help round the family up."

She looked up into his eyes. "You really are a star you know. I love you."

He smiled, but Jade spoke before he got the chance.

"I'm glad you said that. I've been meaning to tell you. Ever since you moved in here with Austin, you got your shine back, sis."

Amber couldn't help but smile. "I feel like I have." She reached up and kissed him. "Thanks to you."

He hugged her to him. "You're the brightest star in my world. I don't mind telling you that."

Dallas leaned in on the other side of him. "I have to tell you, you found yourself a good wife."

Amber gave him a puzzled look. She hoped he wasn't being mean.

Austin turned and punched him arm. "You're just jealous because I'm taking care of Amber now and not you."

Dallas laughed. "Nah. I'll miss it, but you two deserve each other. You're perfect together."

"Thank you."

~ ~ ~

Austin's heart was overflowing with happiness. He couldn't believe that he'd managed to pull this together as quickly as he had. When Amber's dad, Bill had told him how disappointed he was that Austin hadn't come to him first, it had killed him. He would have if he'd had the chance, and he'd realized in that moment that that was his chance. To ask for his permission and to clear everything up in one go.

He glanced over at Bill. He wasn't nearly as bad as Amber thought he was. He hoped that they'd become close given time. There was one thing he was still uncomfortable about, though. Bill had asked him why he'd gone along with a lie, and he'd told him about Milo's phone call. He'd gone with the G-rated version, but Bill hadn't bought it. He'd asked the same thing Amber had—to tell him word for word.

When he did that, he'd thought that Bill might explode, but he'd put a lid on it after a few moments and gotten caught up in the excitement of trying to pull the surprise together. Austin had wanted to ask her right away because that was the only way he could make it all right for her.

Bill came to stand beside him, and they watched Amber and her mom chat with Austin's mom. "Thank you, son."

Austin smiled at him. "Thank you."

"We'll get up here to visit more now."

Lenny came to stand next to Bill. "You won't come to see me, but you'll come to see your new son-in-law?"

Austin tensed. He had the impression that there was no love lost between the two of them.

To his relief, Bill smiled. "Maybe it's taken my new son-in-law to wake me up to a few things."

"What things?"

"Things like the way I've treated my daughters—and my mom."

Lenny smiled. "Maybe it wasn't a one-way street."

Bill nodded.

Austin loved to think that this might bring them closer.

Amber came to him and he slung his arm around her shoulders and dropped a kiss on her lips.

Lenny smiled at them. "Aren't you glad I told you to go along with it?"

Austin raised an eyebrow. "You're not going to tell me that you knew it'd work out this way?"

She laughed. "I didn't even hope it would work out this well this soon. I just knew I didn't want you to walk away because of all the drama."

He hugged Amber closer. "I was never going to walk away."

"Aww." Amber's mom smiled at him. "You gave my little star her shine back."

Amber looked up into his eyes. "I told you. And you're my star."

He chuckled. "If you say so."

Bill brought his phone out and looked down at it. Then he smiled.

"Put that away, Bill. Whatever it is can wait," said her mom.

Bill smiled at Austin. "No. This is important."

"What?"

"I fired Milo."

Amber stared at him. "What about the—"

Bill held a hand up. "I don't want anything to do with him anymore." He met Austin's gaze and mouthed, *thank you.*

~ ~ ~

It was late by the time everyone had gone. Austin held his arms out to her, and Amber went to lean against him.

"Thank you. For telling them. For sorting everything out. For getting everyone here. For …" She looked up into his eyes. "For loving me."

He dropped a kiss on her lips. "I do love you, Amber. I always will." He took hold of her hand and tapped the ring on her finger. "You're going to be my wife."

She smiled. "And you're going to be my husband."

He nodded happily. "Forever."

Roscoe came to join them and stuck his nose up Amber's skirt. She laughed and pushed him away. "Will you ever stop doing that?"

Austin shook his head. "I don't think he will. He loves you almost as much as I do, and I love him for bringing you to me that night."

She tightened her arms around his waist. "I suppose I can let him stick his head up there occasionally—just to show my gratitude."

Austin laughed and took her hand. "In that case. Come with me."

"Where are we going?"

"To bed."

"You wanted to thank me, too, right?"

She laughed. "I do."

He stopped when they reached the bedroom door. "And we can say those words whenever you want to. I don't want to rush or push you, but just so you know, I'm ready whenever you are."

She looped her arms up around his neck and kissed him. She couldn't believe how lucky she was to be the girl he wanted to marry;

;

# A Note from SJ

I hope you enjoyed Austin and Amber's story. Please let your friends know about the books if you feel they would enjoy them as well. It would be wonderful if you would leave me a review, I'd very much appreciate it.

Check out the "Also By" page to see if any of my other series appeal to you – I have a couple of ebook freebie series starters, too, so you can take them for a test drive.

There are a few options to keep up with me and my imaginary friends:

The best way is to Sign up for my Newsletter at my website www.SJMcCoy.com. Don't worry I won't bombard you! I'll let you know about upcoming releases, share a sneak peek or two and keep you in the loop for a couple of fun giveaways I have coming up :0)

You can join my readers group to chat about the books or like my Facebook Page www.facebook.com/authorsjmccoy
I occasionally attempt to say something in 140 characters or less(!) on Twitter

And I'm in the process of building a shiny new website at www.SJMcCoy.com

I love to hear from readers, so feel free to email me at SJ@SJMcCoy.com if you'd like. I'm better at that! :0)

I hope our paths will cross again soon. Until then, take care, and thanks for your support—you are the reason I write!

Love

SJ

# PS Project Semicolon

You may have noticed that the final sentence of the story closed with a semi-colon. It isn't a typo. Project Semi Colon is a non-profit movement dedicated to presenting hope and love to those who are struggling with depression, suicide, addiction and self-injury. Project Semicolon exists to encourage, love and inspire. It's a movement I support with all my heart.

*"A semicolon represents a sentence the author could have ended, but chose not to. The sentence is your life and the author is you."* - Project Semicolon

This author started writing after her son was killed in a car crash. At the time I wanted my own story to be over, instead I chose to honour a promise to my son to write my 'silly stories' someday. I chose to escape into my fictional world. I know for many who struggle with depression, suicide can appear to be the only escape. The semicolon has become a symbol of support, and hopefully a reminder – Your story isn't over yet

# Also by SJ McCoy

**Summer Lake Silver**
Clay and Marianne in Like Some Old Country Song
Seymour and Chris in A Dream Too Far
Ted and Audrey in A Little Rain Must Fall
Diego and Izzy in Where the Rainbow Ends

**Summer Lake Seasons**
Angel and Luke in Take These Broken Wings
Zack and Maria in Too Much Love to Hide
Logan and Roxy in Sunshine Over Snow
Ivan and Abbie in Chase the Blues Away
Austin and Amber in Tell the Stars to Shine

**Summer Lake Series**
Love Like You've Never Been Hurt (FREE in ebook form)
Work Like You Don't Need the Money
Dance Like Nobody's Watching
Fly Like You've Never Been Grounded
Laugh Like You've Never Cried
Sing Like Nobody's Listening
Smile Like You Mean It
The Wedding Dance
Chasing Tomorrow
Dream Like Nothing's Impossible
Ride Like You've Never Fallen
Live Like There's No Tomorrow
The Wedding Flight

# About the Author

I'm SJ, a coffee addict, lover of chocolate and drinker of good red wines. I'm a lost soul and a hopeless romantic. Reading and writing are necessary parts of who I am. Though perhaps not as necessary as coffee! I can drink coffee without writing, but I can't write without coffee.

I grew up loving romance novels, my first boyfriends were book boyfriends, but life intervened, as it tends to do, and I wandered down the paths of non-fiction for many years. My life changed completely a few years ago and I returned to Romance to find my escape.

I write 'Sweet n Steamy' stories because to me there is enough angst and darkness in real life. My favorite romances are happy escapes with a focus on fun, friendships and happily-ever-afters, just like the ones I write.

These days I live in beautiful Montana, the last best place. If I'm not reading or writing, you'll find me just down the road in the park - Yellowstone. I have deer, eagles and the occasional bear for company, and I like it that way :0)

Made in the USA
Middletown, DE
04 August 2020

14366266R00144